CRAIG MARTELLE
MICHAEL ANDERLE

NOMAD FOUND

A KUTHERIAN GAMBIT SERIES
TERRY HENRY WALTON CHRONICLES
BOOK 1

DEDICATION

To Family, Friends and
Those Who Love
To Read.
May We All Enjoy Grace
To Live The Life We Are
Called.

Nomad Found
The Terry Henry Walton Chronicles
Team Includes

BETA / EDITOR BOOK
Acknowledgements in Back!

JIT Beta Readers - From both of us, our deepest gratitude!
Brent Bakken
Mickey Cocker
Simon Hovat
Peter Johnsen
Blk Mrkt
Thomas Ogden
Melissa Ratcliffe
Harry Rothsteni

*If I missed anyone, **please** let me know!*

COPYRIGHT

THE TERRY HENRY WALTON CHRONICLES

THE KUTHERIAN GAMBIT SERIES

Book 1 – Nomad Found (Out)
Book 2 – Nomad Redeemed (Jan 2017)
Book 3 - Nomad Unleashed (2017)
Book 4 - Nomad Supreme (2017)

FREE TRADER SERIES

Book 1 – The Free Trader of Warren Deep
Book 2 – The Free Trader of Planet Vii
Book 3 – Adventures on RV Traveler
Book 4 – Battle for the Amazon
Book 5 – Free the North!
Book 6 – Free Trader on the High Seas
Book 7 – Southern Discontent (January 2017)
Book 8 – The Great 'Cat Rebellion (2017)
Book 9 – Return to the Traveler (2017)

CYGNUS SPACE OPERA - SET IN THE FREE TRADER UNIVERSE

Book 1 – Cygnus Rising
Book 2 – Cygnus Expanding (2017)
Book 3 – Cygnus Arrives (2017)

END TIMES ALASKA SERIES,
A WINLOCK PRESS PUBLICATION

Book 1: Endure
Book 2: Run
Book 3: Return
Book 4: Fury

RICK BANIK THRILLERS

People Raged and the Sky Was on Fire
The Heart Raged (2017)

SHORT STORY CONTRIBUTIONS TO ANTHOLOGIES

Earth Prime Anthology, Volume 1
(Stephen Lee & James M. Ward)
Apocalyptic Space Short Story Collection
(Stephen Lee & James M. Ward)
Lunar Resorts Anthology, Volume 2
(Stephen Lee & James M. Ward)
Just One More Fight
(published as a novella standalone)
The Expanding Universe, Volume 1
(edited by Craig Martelle)
The Misadventures of Jacob Wild McKilljoy
(with Michael-Scott Earle)

KUTHERIAN GAMBIT SERIES TITLES INCLUDE:

FIRST ARC

Death Becomes Her (01) - Queen Bitch (02) - Love Lost (03) - Bite This (04) - Never Forsaken (05) - Under My Heel (06) - Kneel Or Die (07)

SECOND ARC

We Will Build (08) - It's Hell To Choose (09) - Release The Dogs of War (10) - Sued For Peace (11) - We Have Contact (12) - My Ride is a Bitch (13) - Don't Cross This Line (14)

THIRD ARC *(Due 2017)*

Never Submit (15) - Never Surrender (16) - Forever Defend (17) - Might Makes Right (18) - Ahead Full (19) - Capture Death (20) - Life Goes On (21)

New Series

THE SECOND DARK AGES

The Dark Messiah (01)
(Michael's Return)

THE BORIS CHRONICLES
With Paul C. Middleton

Evacuation
Retaliation
Revelation (*Dec 2016*)
Restitution (*2017*)

RECLAIMING HONOR
With Justin Sloan

Justice Is Calling (01)
Claimed By Honor (02)
Jan 2017

THE ETHERIC ACADEMY
With TS Paul

ALPHA CLASS (01) (*Dec 2016/Jan 2017*)
ALPHA CLASS (02) (*Feb/Mar 2017*)
ALPHA CLASS (03) (*May/June 2017*)

TERRY HENRY "TH" WALTON CHRONICLES
With Craig Martelle

See above!

SHORT STORIES

Frank Kurns Stories of the Unknownworld 01 (*7.5*)
You Don't Mess with John's Cousin

Frank Kurns Stories of the Unknownworld 02 (*9.5*)
Bitch's Night Out

ANTHOLOGIES

Glimpse
Honor in Death
(Michael's First Few Days)

Beyond the Stars: At Galaxy's Edge
Tabitha's Vacation

CRAIG MARTELLE SOCIAL

For a chance to see ALL of Craig's new Book Series
Check out his website below!

Website:
http://www.craigmartelle.com

Email List:
http://www.craigmartelle.com
(Go 1/2 way down his first page, the box is in the center!)

Facebook Here:
https://www.facebook.com/AuthorCraigMartelle/

MICHAEL ANDERLE SOCIAL

Website:
http://kurtherianbooks.com/

Email List:
http://kurtherianbooks.com/email-list/

Facebook Here:
https://www.facebook.com/TheKurtherianGambitBooks/

PROLOGUE

He came from the wasteland, broken and dying.

All he wanted was a drink.

But the old lady took him in, because he had kind eyes. She gave him water, food, and a bed.

Within a day, he started helping around the house. Then he straightened her yard, made things the way they were before.

Then the others came, not to ask but to take.

They didn't expect to find a man at her place.

Four arrived. The man walked out into the yard standing tall, giving the others a chance to leave. They didn't. With confidence, he walked into the middle of them and made them pay. He didn't kill them, only beat them mercilessly.

To send a message of "no more" to the other takers.

The old lady watched it all.

When it was over, she walked out to her porch and asked

the man, "Why would you fight them like that?" She nodded to the rapidly disappearing group.

He answered over his shoulder, never taking his eyes off the direction the men left. "Because you gave me water when I was thirsty, and you asked for nothing in return. As long as I live—" He turned to look her in the eye. "—I will be here for you."

"But I don't even know your name," she said.

"Terry Henry Walton, ma'am, but my friends call me TH," he replied.

"How many friends call you TH?" she pried.

"Counting you?" He reached up to wipe the sweat from his forehead. "That would be one."

CHAPTER
ONE

Margie Rose wanted to believe. She wanted to believe that people could be nice again. She couldn't take her eyes off the dark stranger who'd fought for her. She watched him fight and knew that he was never in danger. The only risk was that they would come back and attack her when TH wasn't there.

Bullies worked that way. If they found someone who stood up to them, they'd get their revenge.

"What if they come back?" Margie Rose asked the man, the stranger who had just put himself between her and danger.

He stopped his surveillance of the area around her home and turned to her, his eyes blue…or were they green? "Don't you worry about that. I'm going to pay them a visit long before they are in any shape to return," he told her noncommittally.

Margie remained skeptical. "And what are you going to do then?" she pressed.

He snorted, as much to himself as to her. "I'm going to show them how unhealthy it would be to continue such a lifestyle, and not just for them, but for their families, too, if they have them."

His voice seemed to drop a little, go deeper, but more personal. "In my life, ma'am, I've dealt with bullies and there really are only two ways to get them to stop. The first is to just kill them, but that doesn't necessarily stop the next guy. The second is to make them so afraid that they run screaming whenever they think about confronting you again. Bullies can sense each other, so they'll know. All of them will know that they don't want to come here. Good people will feel safe where bullies are afraid."

He paused and turned back to her. "I'm just going to talk with them, that's all." Terry smiled, his teeth still straight and white, after all the years in the wastelands. His eyes sparkled as his smile lines wrinkled.

"I feel safe just for having known you. Thank you, Mr. Terry Henry Walton. Dinner's in a couple hours." A small smile played at the corner of her lips. "If you could rustle a rabbit, then it will be that much better," Margie Rose said, stabbing a finger toward a stand of shrub not far off.

Terry breathed deeply of the cooling air off the Colorado foothills.

When Chinese code, embedded in billions of net-connected devices, took down the internet by disabling most technology, the world fell quickly. Nukes were tossed about as a disconnected world heaved in its own death throes. Eighty-seven percent of the world's population died from radiation, disease, famine.

Terry disappeared into the mountains once everything he cared about was gone. He swore off the human race. For twenty years he stayed away, but then the Werewolves came and he ran. He only escaped them by leaping from a cliff into a river far below. They were unnaturally fast, unerring in their ability to hunt a human, and unmerciful in their attacks.

As he ran from them, they killed deer and even a bear without hesitation, drank the creatures' blood and resumed their casual hunt for him. Terry had never felt fear like that before. He'd battled with men, and sometimes he thought he would die at their hands, but he hadn't been afraid. The paranormal made his skin crawl. He'd known the stories of the Unknown World from his contact with Dan Bosse of TQB, but really? Well, really deep down, he had hoped to never again have to deal with them in his life.

When he had finally crawled from the river, exhausted from fighting the currents and bashing against rocks, the Werewolves were a long ways away. Terry had staggered to a cabin on the outskirts of a small town. What drew him there were the lights. The town had power, something he hadn't seen in twenty years.

To him, that meant civilization, if only on a limited scale.

Terry would find who was in charge of the town and help that person, even if he or she didn't want help.

That would be Terry's challenge.

But twenty years prior, before the fall, he was smooth, professional. He only had to dig deep and find that person, pull him past the years when he had been barely more than an animal.

Terry looked at the brush, considering his musings before he walked up to this little cabin. Maybe the new Terry Henry Walton could be both professional and a bit animal.

He felt good fighting those men. It had been too long since he sparred, too long since he led men into combat, too long since he'd made a difference for others.

Then the shame washed over him in a wave of grief, from being selfish, running away to survive on his own, letting all the others fend for themselves. He'd started to hate himself. Now he had a shot at redemption. It began with Margie Rose, then one at a time, he'd show people that if they wanted a better world, they had to help each other create it themselves. The town had power, but were they using it to help everyone?

Tomorrow would be a big day. First, he had a rabbit to kill. He pulled a well-used throwing knife, released the hunter within, and stalked upwind toward the brush. With barely a whisper of the wind, he waited. With the rabbit's movement, Terry twisted and flicked. The knife spun through the air, driving through the rabbit's neck for an instant kill.

Terry waited.

Sometimes he wasn't the only predator, so he watched and listened, sniffing the air carefully for any sign. Certain there was nothing, he quickly cleaned his kill, leaving the guts within a snare just in case a coyote appeared. He didn't want to waste good bait and tomorrow's meal.

He hadn't survived in the wild all that time by not shifting the odds in his favor. He believed in making his own luck. He suspected he'd have to change a few attitudes.

Just like he'd do with the trash that had stopped by earlier. Tomorrow, he'd take care of business and put this town on a new track.

❖ ❖ ❖

Billy Spires had been the son of a nobody in a uniquely crappy trailer park full of nobodies. He was average, in both height and looks, and would never stand out in a crowd. His claim to fame was that he was street smart.

For all the good it did him growing up.

He hated that park. He stayed away as much as he could, learned to hunt and kill on his own. Some called him trailer trash, but after the fall, they begged him for help. He was the only one eating. He told them no, except for the women.

He helped them, but they paid a steep price.

Then he found that he could control people by controlling the food. He gathered followers and soon he had a small town beholden to him. Then he discovered an engineer and a mechanic.

The two of those promised him a return to technology, starting with electricity. A freezer to store his venison, his other prizes, and make the food last longer.

So he secreted the two men away, sending women to them on occasion as rewards for their successes, and started to build a real town on the outskirts of what used to be Boulder, Colorado. The mountainous backdrop kept Billy humble.

Well, in his own mind, that was.

From the hills to the west came game and from the fields to the east came grain and vegetables. Billy had evolved from being a street tough to the city planner, the mayor, and the chief justice. There were no elections, nor would there ever be. To Billy, his idea of a benevolent dictator was the best these people could hope for.

Billy sat in the great room of his mansion, looking at the boards he'd set up to track his logistics. He shook his head and laughed, looking around to catch the twinkle in Felicity's eye. She was his southern belle. A new addition to the town.

She'd come willingly to him, which made him suspicious. His only allure was power. A chance encounter with a bobcat left a scar across his left cheek, giving him a personal sneer.

The older he got, the more wary of people he became. He figured he should have killed her because she made him feel funny. He knew he was being manipulated, but found himself agreeing with her recommendations, always to see the sparkle in her eye.

"Get over here, bitch," Billy growled, trying his best to maintain his dominance. She raised an eyebrow at him and continued to stand there, looking at him. "I said get over here!" he screamed, standing to punctuate his anger.

"Now, Billy dear," she said slowly, letting her southern accent drag the words out as she slowly stood up. "It's really okay to let your nice man out every once in a while. He's such a handsome devil. Before you know it, the people will appreciate you like I do, because they'll get to know you. Not quite like I do, though, will they, Billy dear?" She smiled shyly and walked casually, sideways in front of him, highlighting her profile. Her curves were perfect, unlike anything he'd seen since before the fall. The way she filled out her jeans made for a perfect fit in his hand. He looked down, confused, looking at his hand and wondering why it wasn't cupping her butt at that moment.

He was used to his orders being followed. He'd had men killed for less. But not Felicity. He tried to think back to when she simply did what he asked and couldn't find a single instance. It was always the second time that she did what he wanted, after he had changed what he asked for. She confused him, but the rewards kept him coming back.

"Fuck me," he finally said, throwing his hands up as he surrendered to her will. "What do you want?" he asked, rougher than he intended.

"The electricity, Billy dear. When will it flow to all the houses in town? When can we fire up the refinery? I, for one, would love to ride. Walking is so last century." She approached him slowly, smiling. He couldn't help himself as he smiled back.

❖ ❖ ❖

"I feel like shit," the oldest of the friends gasped through gritted teeth. "Fuck that guy! He can't do that to us." James was the largest of the bunch and had taken the worst of the beatings. He nursed his ribs, wincing at the pain that coursed through his entire body. Beside one half-swollen eye, his face was unharmed.

The others weren't as lucky as that.

"Shut up, Jim. He can and he did. The real question is what are we going to do about it?" Mark asked them, lisping as he talked through two loose teeth and split and swollen lips.

Mark was unrecognizable from the man he'd been just a day earlier. Terry had mercilessly pounded on the man's head because he kept talking, insulting the old lady, and denying that he'd lost the fight. Terry sent him a personal message.

"I think my jaw's broke," the third man slurred while trying to rub it with bandaged fingers. He had tried taking a swing at Terry, but it was blocked and his fingers dislocated as part of the countermove that saw him put face first in the dirt. He wasn't too proud to realize he had just had his ass kicked.

He had laid there and whimpered.

The fourth man, the leader called John, was just crawling from his bed. He moved slowly as if he were eighty-years old. "What are we going to do about it? Three days, then we go back, pay them a visit in the middle of the night, burn the house down around them. We can't have anyone standing up to us. Billy's been thinking he's losing control of those on the outskirts, and we need to send a message. We can't have people fighting back, so they need to die. The old lady and especially that man."

"Yeah! Let's go fuck some shit up!" Jim cheered. John looked at him and shook his head. He considered himself better than this rabble, but these were the men that Billy gave him to work with, and no one crossed Billy, not if you wanted peace in your life.

And food.

Maybe he'd let that man knock off one or two of these idiots before he was put down. That would be a win-win. John had a few days to figure out how to make that work. He knew he'd come up with something.

He always did.

❖ ❖ ❖

The gray wolf was silent, unseen in the forest.

Marcus sniffed the air and lowered down on his haunches. He, and the rest of his group, could smell the deer ahead of them. The wind bringing their scent, and keeping them hidden from their prey.

Now, if they didn't screw up, he and the guys were going to eat well this evening.

For the last four hours he, Ted, Simmons, Adams, and Merrit had been reveling in their Were forms, chasing rabbits and laughing at each other. It had been a good way to blow off some extra energy out in the wild. A chance to get away and enjoy themselves.

Now, they needed to bring home a couple of deer and placate the girls or their asses were going to be grass and the ladies would bring the lawn mowers. They might as well stay out all night. He chuffed, maybe that wouldn't be a bad idea? No, no good there. No real reason and the bitching would be twice as bad in the morning.

The team took ten minutes to get closer. He snuggled lower, his mouth salivating at the thought of fresh deer.

BAM!

Marcus's head turned in the direction of the gunshot and then quickly back towards the deer. DAMMIT! The deer had bolted and… THERE!

He started growling, and the four others in his group growled as well.

The human hunter looked in their direction, his eyes growing wide in surprise before narrowing. Turning around and then back to looking at Marcus and his four Were brothers, it looked like he was calculating.

The man turned and ran away from the group. Marcus and his team broke from their cover. The chase was on!

Just like a couple days ago with the other human, but that one had the decency not to scare off the game before he jumped off the cliff. They could see he'd survived the fall to the river below when he came back up, sputtering, but chasing him wasn't worth it.

This time, it damn sure was.

Marcus waved his snout in one direction and then the other. Ted and Adams spread out to the right and sprinted, well beyond the hunter's avenue of escape. Simmons and Merrit went left, doing the same thing. Marcus raced straight down the gut, chasing the hunter, who realized his peril too late.

He turned to fire. Marcus dodged as he ran, foiling the aim. A round skipped past him, one blew over his head, and the last shot, as he closed in on the human, caught him high in the shoulder. Marcus howled his fury as he jumped with the full force of his Were strength, hitting the man chest high and sending him flying into a tree. The hunter crumpled to the ground, barely breathing.

The other four Werewolves closed and encircled the man, but Marcus held them back. He was injured and for that, he'd drink his fill of the human's blood before the others tore him apart. They would rend his flesh just because.

It sent a good message to those who might think they could hunt where the predator would become the prey. Marcus bit deeply into the man's throat and savored the copper tint of fresh blood. It had been a while since he'd feasted on a human.

He had found a few years ago that he liked it.

And wanted more.

CHAPTER TWO

Terry Henry Walton woke early after a sound four hours of sleep. In the wild, he'd gotten used to sleeping in smaller chunks of time. When he had his dog, a rescued wolf actually, he'd slept soundly as the beast would watch. But finally the big, shaggy creature lost his battle with old age. Terry had loved that dog.

Ever since, he'd felt a certain loneliness. Maybe if he established himself here, he'd get another dog. They were more trustworthy than people. They wanted so very little but gave everything they had.

So with that thought to keep him warm, he silently left Margie Rose's house while she was asleep and it was still dark, long before the false dawn.

He'd found out where the men lived, deciding that getting the information from the townsfolk would have been harder than simply tracking them down by their footprints and blood trails. He was impressed at how much blood marked the trail.

He figured they were still incapable of wiping their snotty noses without help. He chuckled to himself thinking about how they sniveled afterwards, dragging themselves away after the worst beating of their lives. Four against one. Terry figured they needed another ten to even things out.

When he arrived at their house inside the town's boundary, he found that lights were on. He crouched and approached tactically, keeping his throwing knife at the ready. A woman was inside moving around, clanking pans and sounding like she was preparing breakfast. *Good*, Terry thought. *They need to know that their families will die horrible deaths if they ever hassle Margie Rose again.*

Terry sat below the window and listened, sneaking peeks when the footsteps walked away. Table, chairs, an old ratty couch, doors to various rooms. No one visible beside an older lady wearing an apron. He wondered which one's mother she was, or maybe all of them with four different fathers. One never knew in this world, and Terry didn't care. It wasn't his place to care, only to know where he could find the best leverage.

He went from window to window, building a map of the home's interior within his mind and coming up with a plan for one man to overwhelm five. Surprise was on his side, but that wouldn't make the statement he wanted.

He waited.

They awoke, one by one, and stumbled into the main area of the house. The last one out, the man they called John, backhanded the old lady because she wasn't quick enough bringing his breakfast.

She cowered as she returned to the stove for a new plate.

That put Terry over the edge. He felt the rage surge into him and he started running around the corner of the cabin. Swinging wide to gain speed and hitting the door with a two-footed jump, both feet smashing into the door next to the knob.

It crashed open and he landed roughly, recovered quickly. With surprising speed, he crossed the room and leapt over the table, catching John's head in his hands as he passed.

Terry landed behind John, twisted as he still held the man's head. He rotated his trunk, yanking John out of his chair. As the man was falling, Terry jerked back and snapped the man's neck. Terry let go of the man's corpse, dropping him to the floor as he turned in a crouch and pulled a knife into each hand.

"Holy fuck, he killed John!" Jim blurted, his wide eyes darting back and forth between the man and his friends. "Did you see that? Holy fuck!"

Mark looked calm, leaning back in his chair as he chewed a pancake. He put his silverware down and held his hands up. After swallowing, he cleared his throat. "Let's not be hasty. John was a bastard. I think Miss Grimes has done more for us than he did, and look how he treated her." He nodded to the old lady, who only glared back.

"Can I get you some breakfast, mister? It would be my pleasure," the older lady said kindly.

Terry glanced in her direction and shook his head before quickly returning his eyes to the three. "No, thank you, ma'am. If you could give us some privacy, I have unfinished business with these three."

"It's been too long," she whispered as she gently ran one hand down Terry's arm. Miss Grimes gathered her things and only stopped a second to admire the ruined door before stepping through. He watched her go, wondering what she meant, before returning his attention to the business at hand.

He leaned down and removed the black leather bullwhip that John had at his belt. He'd tried to use it when they tried to attack Margie Rose's place. Terry had let him keep it because he was too slow with it to be dangerous. But he liked it and felt like he needed it to pay homage to his Indiana Jones namesake.

"Now, where were we? Yes, this is the part where I make you swear upon your mothers' graves that you won't ever return to Miss Margie Rose's house, ever again, for as long as you may live."

He nodded to the dead man on the floor. "If I don't believe you, then we'll measure that second part in minutes. Not a threat, but a promise."

Terry lifted John's chair off the ground, turning it around and sitting with his arms resting on the chair back as he watched the three men intently. He could tell the big one would be a problem as he wasn't smart enough to understand that his size wouldn't get him out of this.

Mark was the new leader and the last one, Devlin, he didn't know enough to be as afraid as he should have been.

"I think that's an easy promise for us to make. You see, tonight we were going to pay you a visit, burn that old house down with you inside. That was John's plan anyway," Mark said, stabbing a finger in disgust toward the body on the floor.

Jim looked aghast. "Why are you telling him our plan, fuckstick?" the large man cried, trying to be threatening, but failing as his voice was an octave higher than it should have been.

Terry understood that to mean that Mark was telling the truth. It was the start of the delicate truth dance, enough to be convincing, but would it be enough for him to drop his guard?

Terry was able to lean over the smaller table and rabbit-punched the big man in the temple. Jim's eyes rolled back, he collapsed with a bang onto the table, and crumpled onto the floor. Mark casually leaned out of the way so Jim wouldn't touch him on his way down.

Devlin's eyes grew wide, but he kept his mouth shut.

"I suspect you have some kind of loose association with the man who runs this town." Mark confirmed with a terse nod. "I need an introduction and then I'd like you two to work for me, and if you can keep him under control, Jim too," Terry dropped his offer on them. Devlin's mouth dropped open. Terry pointed with his knife and flicked the tip to encourage him to close his mouth.

"I can introduce you, but I don't know how he's going to take it. He's used to dealing with us," Mark said smoothly.

"Then dealing with me will be like a breath of fresh air, don't you think? So, shall we?" Terry gestured toward the door. Mark sat still, finally deciding that Billy would probably have the man killed. That would put Mark in charge, so he figured it was a good plan. Devlin couldn't believe what he was seeing.

"Help me," Mark said as he moved to Jim's side and took one arm.

Devlin took the other and mouthed, *what are you doing?*

"What am I doing? I'm not dying. Does that make sense to you? Can you take him?" He nodded toward Terry. Devlin hung his head. Terry stood and walked in front of them so he could look both the men in the face.

"Let me tell you what I see. That man will do what you tell him," Terry said, pointing to Jim's semi-limp form and then to Mark. "You think that your boss will take care of me so you're turning me over to him. And you, you aren't a bully at all. You're the only one who's trying to understand who I am and our relationship. I don't want to have to watch my back. I have to believe that I've convinced you not to fuck with me or I kill you. There is no in between. Do you two think I can kill you?" They both nodded, looking at the knife in Terry's hand that he was using to point with.

"Why don't I just kill you now?" he asked, looking at Devlin. The young man couldn't hold Terry's gaze. His eyes bore into Devlin's soul, making him feel ashamed.

"I don't want to die," the young man finally conceded. Terry used a finger to tip Devlin's head up so he could judge the young man's sincerity. He smiled and nodded.

"Me neither," Mark said with a shrug. Terry pulled him close until their faces were inches apart. He glared at the bully until the man caved. "Let me go, fucker."

"Finally, the first honest thing you've said. I expect your boss will take umbrage at my presence, but I believe that I have a convincing argument. Let's go see who's right."

Terry hesitated for a moment then shook his head as he eyed the two men. "Please don't make me kill you between here and there, as I have no desire to carry Mr. Lumpy. If you do anything, Mark, I'll end up killing you both and do you really want his death on your conscience? Come on, man, buck up. There's a new sheriff in town." Terry slapped Mark on the shoulder hard enough for him to lose his grip on Jim, dropping him to the floor where Devlin was pulled down on top of him.

Terry backed away, laughing as the cursing men struggled to get things back under control. Mark held up his hands as he went to the sink and grabbed a pitcher, carrying it back to the comatose man. He splashed water in Jim's face and growled at him to wake up, putting the pitcher on the table.

The four men left the house and headed toward town. Terry stayed behind them and started whistling happily. Devlin walked proudly, shoulders back and head held high. Mark was skeptical, and Jim was dazed, stumbling along as if returning from an all-night bender.

Must have a thin skull, Terry thought. *They just don't make them like they used to.*

CHAPTER THREE

Billy was in a foul mood. He'd expected better harvests for the first crops. He'd apportioned both water and power to those with greenhouses to help them early-up the growing season. But the reward was minimal. Felicity leaned against him as he sat in his overstuffed chair, stewing as he remembered the last farmer to report.

He'd sent the man away with death threats. He told his men to bodily throw the farmer out the front door, which they dutifully did.

"What the fuck is wrong with these people?!" he howled, slamming his fist on the table. "Wankers!"

Felicity cocked an eyebrow. "Wankers? Where'd you learn that one, dear?" she asked in a soft voice.

"One of those damn foreigners that came through here. It's almost as good as spunkmaster, don't you think?" he said, calming as he thought about the breadth and depth of his colorful vocabulary.

"I wouldn't know anything about that, Billy dear. Maybe we can just call them farmers and not beat them up when the garden doesn't grow. You want him to work hard, don't you? Imagine what he would do if he farmed because he loved it, not because he was afraid of you. He used to love farming, now I expect he's wasting time planning to run away from here."

Billy scoffed, his eyes looking at her before returning to look in front of him. "That's crazy talk, bitch. They need me, far more than I need them. I survived a decade before any of those lazy dirt grubbers showed up. They can all get in a nice long line and suck my balls. And they'll be happy to do it, too."

"Really?" she said, icicles hanging from that one word. Her eyes narrowed as she glared at Billy Spires. He looked at her, then stood and grabbed her arms, shaking her. Her eyes didn't waver from his.

"You don't know what you're talking about," he said in a normal tone, looking away. "They only know fear."

He felt like carrying her to his bed, to show her what he meant, but a knock on the door stalled his hand. He realized that he couldn't have done it. He cared what she thought and as much as she made him spitting mad, he didn't want to hurt her. He was confused, like he'd been from when he first met her.

"I'm not a nice man," he finally committed to saying as he gently let go of her arms. She blinked at him, crystal blue eyes below shining chestnut hair.

"Of course my Billy isn't a nice man. Maybe that's why I'm here…" she drawled, leaving the ending hanging.

❖ ❖ ❖

Terry thought the governor's mansion should have looked more like a mansion. It was barely bigger than a normal house, but it was far busier with people coming and going. Horse-drawn carts were scattered on a road leading east toward the fields.

Consolidation of food was one way to control the people. Terry wondered if he'd have to kill the self-proclaimed mayor and take over. He didn't want that.

But he'd already made his decision. He would do what he had to because in that direction was his redemption.

The people needed him and they didn't even know who he was. That would change soon enough. The four of them approached the front door, where a fat man with a rifle stood guard. Terry wondered if the man could shoot. Bullets were one of the most scarce commodities of the new world. Terry brushed his thoughts aside once he was within arm's reach of the man.

"We need to see Billy," Mark said gruffly.

"I'm not sure you want to see him right now. Go away and come back tomorrow," the man sneered through broken teeth, tipping his head back as he tried to look down on the group. Mark shrugged and started to turn, but Terry was past him and in a move too fast for the eyes to follow, grabbed the rifle and twisted it from the fat man's grip.

Terry backed up as the man protested and started forward. Terry reversed the rifle and butt-stroked the man's face. With his nose ruined, lips split, and face destroyed, the man collapsed.

Bubbles in the blood suggested he wasn't dead, but that wasn't Terry's concern. He opened the door and walked into a small entryway, waving at the other three men to follow him.

The look he gave them suggested they best not double-cross him.

Devlin followed first, in awe at their new acquaintance's skills. "Did you see that?" he asked his two buddies admiringly.

Mark nodded tersely and pushed Jim in front of him.

Terry saw the marks on the floor where the majority of the traffic went. They led to closed double-doors. Terry walked up and knocked boldly, waiting for an answer.

When he heard a shout from within, he opened the doors and waved the others to go in first. Mark hesitated once he saw the look on Billy's face.

"Get in there, dickweed," Terry grumbled. When all three were inside, Terry put the rifle on the table in front of Billy and sat down. Billy's face turned red as he let his anger get the best of him.

"Who in the holy fuck are you?" he demanded, eyes looking at the rifle and then back at the annoying man sitting in his chair.

Terry turned his head slightly and you could hear his neck pop in the stillness of the room. "I'm Terry Henry Walton, and who do I have the pleasure of addressing?" he asked as he noted everything about the man, then looked at the raving beauty who stood at his side.

Terry nodded once in her direction before turning his attention back to the self-appointed mayor. Billy followed the glance and looked quickly to Felicity, seeing that she responded with a slight smile, eyes continuing to sparkle as she looked at the stranger.

Billy lunged for the rifle, grabbing it and aiming at the stranger, he pulled the trigger.

Click.

Terry put his hand on the table and deposited the two

bullets he'd cycled out of the rifle when he was in the entryway. Billy slammed the rifle on the table and remained
standing so he could loom over the other man. Billy looked
at Mark, Jim, and Devlin. Then something registered.

"Where's John?" he asked, his eyes narrowing.

"Tell him," Terry ordered. When Mark started to speak,
Terry stopped him and pointed. "You, Devlin."

"Well, Mr. Spires, we paid the old lady on the outskirts of
town a visit because John said she had some vegetables that
came in." Devlin swallowed and his head bobbed in Terry's
direction, "This man was there and he beat the shit out of
the four of us. Then he shows up this morning by crashing
through the door and ripped John's head off. He told us if we
ever bothered the old lady again, he would kill us. Jim made
a comment I don't think he liked so he beat Jim senseless for
good measure," Devlin shared.

Billy's rage cooled. He hadn't been afraid of John or Jim.
They were punks, but he wouldn't fight all four of them at
once. He studied the newcomer's face. Not a mark. He'd killed
a man with his bare hands and beaten one of the biggest men
in town senseless, and they hadn't touched him.

"I'm Billy Spires," he said. Felicity put a hand on his arm,
and he rested his free hand over hers, subtly telling Terry
Henry Walton that she was a war he didn't want to fight.

Terry had no intention of fighting over her. He recognized her for what she was: the power behind the throne. He
remembered well his studies of history, thinking about Otto
von Bismarck's role in the service of Prussian King William I.
Or closer to home, how Woodrow Wilson's wife ran the government when President Wilson had a stroke. Terry didn't
want the throne, so he didn't want her.

His logic was simple.

MARTELLE AND ANDERLE

"You run the most modern society of any I've seen."
Terry didn't share that he hadn't seen any others since he
retreated to the mountains twenty years prior. "My compli-
ments to you on what you've accomplished. Now, I'm here
because you have a problem. With your success, comes envy.
There are those in the wastelands who will want what you
have, to take it and leave you with nothing. You're counting
on the likes of that fat man out front? Or these guys?" Terry
pointed to three men still standing. Mark knew he should
take offense, but didn't want to get in the middle of the power
struggle.

He still had hopes Billy would have the man killed.

Terry continued, "My offer is simple. I will work for you
as your chief of security. I don't want your position as mayor
or your better half. I want to secure this town so it can grow,
become the basis of a new city-state, a nation-state. I don't
do that management stuff, but you do and you do it well." He
jerked a hand behind him. "I'll train these men and others
like them to protect and defend this town. I will help you
protect your engineers, the people you have to have and who
will flourish with freedom and support."

He paused and added for good measure, "Power for all.
Water for all."

Terry looked at the man before him, watched the wheels
turning. "You're asking yourself if you can trust me," Terry added. "I could have simply shot you the second I came
through the door. You being alive is, in my opinion, the best
solution or I would have simply killed you. The proof, as they
say, was in my actions."

Felicity gripped Billy's arm and leaned close until her lips
touched his ear. He closed his eyes so he could focus on her
caress.

"Accept his offer and then come to my bed and make love to me," she taunted.

Billy's eyes snapped open as he struggled to say the words, finally compromising with himself. "We will do this, temporarily. You'll be my acting security chief until you prove to me that I don't need to have you killed. You have no idea who my people are or when they could strike, and we'll keep it that way." He gestured towards the door. "Off with you now. Go do security stuff. I have business to take care of."

Terry looked from the mayor to Felicity. She winked at the new man when Billy turned away. Without further delay, Terry stood to leave, waving at his comrades.

Billy spoke after getting out of his chair, his hand rubbing Felicity. "Security man, one last thing. One of my hunters went into the hills and never returned. Maybe you can find him for me? He had one of our rifles and a pocket full of ammunition." Terry froze.

"Which hills?" he asked.

"What hills do you think?" Billy sniped. "Due west and a little south. He was going for elk. Took a horse, too. Your stock will rise with me if you can bring him home with his horse and gear," Billy said, not looking at Terry. His eyes were devouring his prize instead. Felicity smiled at Billy, leaving little to the imagination regarding what would happen next. Terry strode briskly from the room, while the others hurried to catch up.

CHAPTER FOUR

Ted, Simmons, Adams, and Merrit stood together in a clearing outside the cabins that had been a camper's retreat in the time before. They stood around a fire pit, but there was no fire. They shuffled their feet and sniffed the summer air. No one knew what to say.

The other Werewolves had tasted the human's flesh. They usually didn't eat humans, but this was a new era and they were a new pack. Marcus liked the taste, but the others weren't sure. Elk was so much better, in their minds. They'd killed one that day, just after the man went down. They barely ate any of his flesh, but left Marcus to his depredations. He was the alpha male and they would do as he directed, but if they had a choice, they were sure they would not dine on human flesh again.

Were they devolving toward a more animalistic Werewolf? What if they stopped changing back to human form?

The other Weres didn't know if that could happen, but watching Marcus, they started to fear. Maybe it was time for a new alpha.

Simmons asked the others to follow him as he walked back into the woods, changing shape into a Werewolf as he went. The fur would keep him warm. Ted, Adam, and Merrit followed as they put as much distance as possible between them and Marcus, who was arguing with his she-wolf.

Simmons didn't want anyone to hear.

❖ ❖ ❖

"Margie Rose! You are a goddess in the kitchen. If I were only a few years younger, I'd be a suitor at your door," Terry jibed as he sat at the table, his plate looking like it had been licked clean. Eggs with leftover rabbit and peppers scrambled together. She'd made pancakes topped with fresh berries from one of the greenhouses.

Terry hadn't eaten real home cooking in forever. He almost felt drunk.

Margie Rose wiped her hands on her apron, feeling good about having Terry in the house. She felt safe and like she had a renewed purpose. She didn't know why, but felt that her responsibility was to take care of him so he could do greater things.

"What do you intend to do here, Mr. Walton?" she asked formally. She would not call him TH. Not yet, anyway.

"What do you mean, Margie Rose?" he asked, letting his eyes roll back in his head from the near orgasmic pleasure of such an incredible meal. All he had to do was provide the foodstuffs and the older lady would turn them into culinary delights. He wanted more of that.

"Let's start with who you are, who you really are. How did you become this person?" She looked at him, smiling, with flour on her apron from making the pancakes. She sat at the table, having not eaten. Terry noticed that she'd given it all to him. He owed her for her blind trust in him and her support. He decided to tell her the truth, well, most of it anyway.

"I used to be in the Marines, then I left after an unfortunate incident, and took private work where we secured some things, hurt some people. Then I returned to working with the Marines. I was married, had a child. After the apocalypse, the war, they died. I bailed out on it all. Ran away to the mountains to hide. Left the world to people like those around here, bullies. I'm so sorry, Margie Rose, that you and people like you had to go it alone. For you and for them, I will spend the rest of my life trying to make up for my disgrace, my running. You deserve to have a good life. I will do what I can to make that happen." Terry's eyes looked green as he gazed at the older woman. All feelings of food euphoria had left him.

Business. He was back into the business of humanity, but this time, he bore the burden alone. He had to build it all from scratch so people like Margie Rose could live in peace. He'd leverage those who'd shown they could be useful, like the four street toughs he'd taught a lesson to, like Billy Spires.

Terry wasn't sure about him, but he lived by the old Mad Dog Mattis adage. Be nice to everyone you meet, but have a plan to kill them. Even though Billy didn't know it, he was living on borrowed time. One reason to keep him alive was to keep Felicity from sniffing around. He'd seen her type before, drawn to men in power.

He wasn't sure about her, either.

There seemed to be something unnatural to her beauty, much like his own. He wondered...

◈ ◈ ◈

"Come on, Billy, let's go visit that nice farmer you had thrown out of here yesterday so you can apologize to him," Felicity drawled, smiling as her fingers played with his full head of brown hair.

"Fuck off!" he exclaimed. She pursed her lips and raised one eyebrow. The temperature in the room dropped ten degrees. Billy shivered and reached for his shirt. They were in bed and naked. He was gratified, but she wanted to talk. She always wanted something.

But what she was willing to pay to get it! Billy had never felt the way she made him feel. All he had to do was be nice to the farmer and then she'd do that little thing where she twisted her hips. Holy shit! His eyes rolled back in his head as he thought about it.

"Sorry," he mumbled when he opened his eyes again. "Let's go do that. It's a nice day for a stroll. We can talk with all of them, tell them that their work is feeding us all. Thank them for taking dirt and water and growing food. That's easy, Felicity, but what are we going to do about him, that Walton guy?"

"We, dear? You can own him, if you don't abuse him. He'll work for you, that's what he said, and he's got honest eyes. I trust him, since you know he could have easily killed you. He chose not to, maybe you should think about that. He will make you great, but he's going to ask you to change. I think you need to listen to him. He won't ask for much, but what he asks for, you'll have to give him. What would it be like if the people here loved you? Maybe you could stop telling everyone to go fuck themselves. That gets old, Billy dear," she said, her voice getting softer and softer as she spoke. She ended with her lips on his neck, nibbling.

He was getting older, and it was tiring to have to always watch his own back. That fat bastard who'd been guarding the door to his house was useless and those were the kind of people he was left with, although he had no choice in that man's case. Blood demanded that he take care of him. He sat up straight in bed and hung his head, his chin resting on his hairless chest.

"God damn it. You're going to make me into a real mayor, aren't you?" He looked at her out of the corner of his eye. She sat up, the sheet falling from her perky, young breasts. She smiled, making no attempt to cover herself. "Next thing you know, I'll be shaking hands, kissing babies, and asking for votes. NO! Don't you even think that. Voting will never fucking happen. I'm the benevolent dictator, growing more benevolent with each day, but I will always be a dictator, Felicity dear," he stated, emphasizing his point by tapping his chest with his thumb.

He climbed out of bed and stretched, exposing himself fully. Felicity rolled her eyes and then mirrored his efforts. "You can't compare, Billy dear," she said as she headed toward the bathroom. It was nice having a pump and running water. A warm shower was better than no shower, she reasoned, but having that, she wanted the hot shower, which meant that all the infrastructure had to be improved. She thought about the lengths she was willing to go for the luxuries she felt that she deserved. Getting Billy to apologize was only so they could get better vegetables.

It was all part of her plan, because she deserved the best.

❖ ❖ ❖

"That must have been hard for you, Mr. Walton," Margie Rose started. "But it's all water under the bridge. I watched my husband die after twenty- years of marriage, ten years after the fall, ten years ago. It seems like forever. I kept going because that's what he would have wanted, but I never really had any hope. Not until now, that is. You've made me believe that people can be good to each other again. All it cost me is a pan of scrambled eggs in the morning and something for dinner? It's a deal, Terry Henry Walton. You keep doing what you're doing and I'll keep doing what I'm doing." She ended by holding out a hand, too thin from not eating enough and calloused from working too hard. Terry carefully pushed his chair back, stood, and walked around until he could pull the old woman to her feet, where he hugged her for a long time. He held her as she cried and then she pushed him away so she could wipe her face on her apron.

Terry laughed at the flour smeared across one cheek. "I have to run across town and find my boys, get them doing something productive, then I need to go into the mountains and look for a hunter who's gone missing. I may not be back tonight, but make no mistake, since you've promised eggs each morning, I will be here for that. I don't think I want to start my day any other way, Margie Rose."

She reached for his plate, but he stopped her and took it to the sink himself. He held up the drying rag, pointing at her to do the washing. Clean up was easy with two people. Five minutes later, Terry bolted out the front door and easily jogged the two miles to the house his boys occupied. He hoped that they hadn't gotten into any trouble.

When he arrived, the front door had not been repaired. He leaned his head in and saw Mrs. Grimes cleaning up the kitchen. She waved when she saw him.

"Where are they?"

"They ate their breakfast and went back to bed," she said happily. Terry was angry, but not at her. He crossed the room casually, smiling, then roped her into a big hug. He grabbed the drying rag and for the second time that morning, he dried the dishes. She tried to shoo him away, but he would have none of it. He also wanted to cool down as he didn't want to kill his new recruits. The boys needed a few days before he'd determine that they needed to die, and then he'd kill them one by one, Maybe by the time he got to the last one, that man would understand and be more accommodating.

"Mark?" he asked and Mrs. Grimes pointed to one door. "Jim?" The next door. "Devlin?" She pointed again. As he was thinking who to rouse first, Devlin's door opened and he walked out, fully dressed and ready to go.

"I thought I heard you, Terry," he said as he approached. Terry raised his eyebrows and turned his head sideways. "I mean, Mr. Walton," Devlin quickly corrected. Terry relaxed and nodded.

"Wait here, please," he told the young man. Terry crossed the dining area and tried to turn the knob to Mark's room. It was locked. He rocked back and with one foot, kicked the door, breaking the jamb, and the door flew open.

Mark sat up in bed. He was awake. If Terry wasn't mistaken, he thought Mark was slapping the blue buffalo.

"Well, Mark. You do have a soft side," Terry said. "One-eyed Willie letting you down?"

"Get out!" the man shouted, but softened when he saw the murderous look in Terry's eye, the good humor of his jibes vanishing instantly. "I'm sorry. Can't a man have a little peace? Let me get dressed and I'll be right out."

Terry decided not to kill Mark right then, but every day

was a new day. For the smart one of the group, he wasn't very smart. Terry left the door wide open and walked to Jim's room, tapping gently on it with one knuckle. Before the third rap, the door was yanked open and Jim jumped at him.

Terry rotated on the balls of his feet and let Jim's momentum carry him past. With a helping hand and a turn of his hips, Terry drove Jim head first into the wall of the hallway. Before he could stand up to shake out the cobwebs, Terry dropped straight down, driving an elbow into the middle of the big man's back. He gasped as the air was driven from his lungs and he collapsed. He weakly reached out an arm, trying to wrap it around Terry's leg. Terry kicked Jim in the face and the man stopped his struggling.

"One more time, Jim, and you die. Get that through your thick skull. I need your help. I need your strength, but it's no good to me if you're dead, buried face down on top of John. Do you understand that?" Jim nodded almost imperceptibly. "Now get up and get yourself cleaned up. You're not hurt that badly." Terry stepped over the prone figure and walked down the hallway, almost running into Mark as he emerged from his room, still buttoning his rough shirt. Terry leaned close. "Go help him. If he tries to attack me again, I'll assume that you are making him do it, because you're too much of a candy ass to do it yourself. And then I'll kill you both. You show me that you can lead these men, starting with the dumb one back there." Terry stabbed a thumb down the hallway to highlight who he meant, just in case Mark was confused.

Terry glared at Mark, who quickly looked away. *Good*, Terry thought.

The alpha male had spoken and the pups had just peed themselves.

CHAPTER FIVE

Once he had all three men outside, Terry taught them about calisthenics and fitness. Devlin followed along willingly, but Mark was more reluctant, until getting cuffed in the head, then his motivation greatly improved. Jim stumbled along as well as he could. When Terry looked at his eyes, he realized that maybe he'd kicked Jim in the head one too many times. He suspected the big man had a concussion.

Or two.

So they put him on bed rest, which he didn't understand right away, until Mark explained it to him. Mrs. Grimes agreed to take care of him and Terry committed to sending extra food home with the boys, but they were going to be gone for a while.

Terry told them to grab their travel bags. They had simple bags that they slung over one shoulder. They carried water and a little hard bread, a thin blanket, an extra shirt, and pair of socks.

Terry carried his knives, his new bullwhip that he took from John, and that was it. He looked forward to the time when he'd have a rifle and a pistol again. He hoped that time would come soon. He felt almost invincible when packing firepower.

They headed west on the main trail heading out of town toward the mountains. Terry hoped to pick up the hunter's track and trail him into the hills. He was afraid at what he'd find, not the body of a hunter, but the Werewolves. He'd barely escaped with his life last time, and they weren't even hunting him. He knew better than to cross Weres and would stay as far away from them as he could. Dragging the two delinquents would make that more difficult, but they needed an indoctrination on what it meant to work for him.

He laughed to himself as he walked briskly. Devlin was keeping up, but Mark was panting heavily and falling back. "Get up here!" Terry growled at the man, barely turning his head to acknowledge Mark's transgression of discipline and self-motivation. To Mark's credit, he jogged to catch back up, and then skip-ran every few steps to stay even with the other two. After a mile of that, Terry slowed his pace, then called a halt so he could let his men rest. They had not yet reached the end of the road, but he needed to concentrate and he couldn't have the heavy breathing of his boys draw the wolves. Or their clumsiness in the woods.

"Truth time, gentlemen," Terry opened as a way of getting their attention. They drank sparingly of their water and ate some bread, while giving him the rest of their focus. "There are creatures in these mountains beyond anything you've ever encountered before. Have you ever heard of Werewolves?"

He expected them to nod, but they didn't. They shrugged. He realized that they were in their mid to late-twenties, just children during the fall. They grew up without knowing movies, or reading books.

"Can you read?" he asked suddenly. Mark nodded while Devlin shook his head. That made things clear. He added that to his mental to-do list. They needed a school. Civilization would rise because of education. The future generations would have to lead the way ahead, because not everyone would be there forever. Not everyone was a vampire or a Were creature.

If humanity stood a chance, it was through a return to a modern civilization.

"Werewolves are creatures of supernatural power. No human can stand up to one, not even a human with a rifle. We go up there, find the hunter, and then we get the hell out. No sightseeing, no loitering. The longer we're there, the more we risk drawing attention to ourselves. I think they've migrated into this area, and nothing good will come of it. So, gentlemen, I need you to move like a light breeze, make no noise, disturb no undergrowth. Do you think you could do that for me?" Terry didn't expect an answer and he didn't get one. The two men simply looked at him.

He was asking too much. "Do you two want to go back?"

"No!" Devlin said adamantly. Mark hung his head.

"I don't want you to think I'm a pussy, but reality says, I don't know dick about moving quietly in the brush." He nodded at Devlin, "And neither does Mr. Gung Ho here. We'd be a liability if what you think is up there happens to be waiting. Sure, if you got yourself killed, I wouldn't shed a tear for you, but we all know that your best chance is by going alone," Mark said calmly, holding Terry with his gaze as he spoke.

"That's the smartest thing you've said since I've known you," Terry replied. "And you're right. You two head back, but what I want you to do is go to one of the greenhouses and help them. Learn something about farming and get your hands dirty. You could blow me off, expecting that I won't return, but what if I do? What do you think I'll do to you when I find out? And you know I'm going to check, because you're going to take me, tomorrow morning after I've come to collect you. I promised Miss Margie Rose that I would meet her for breakfast and by God, I keep my promises." Terry smacked his hand with his fist, physically driving home his point. He looked at both men for an instant, turned, and started running down the road. To Mark and Devlin, it seemed like he was sprinting, but Terry knew that he could maintain that world-class pace for a long time.

The nanocytes in his blood helped him, enough to heighten his abilities and tweak his senses. He always felt strong because of them, but knew that there was so much more. Vampires and Werewolves would laugh at him and tear him apart without breaking a sweat.

Terry continued. Fear would do him no good. He found the hunter's trail easily and followed it uphill.

❖ ❖ ❖

Marcus was tired of fighting with the old lady. When he dragged himself out of the cabin, he found the pack males had gone. He was mad already and this made him angrier. They would be the target of his ire. He sniffed the air and reached out with his senses, feeling that they weren't nearby. He changed to his Werewolf form and sniffed the ground, finding their scent and racing after them.

His anger built as he ran, and he started to growl. The cool air of the late-morning July sun did nothing to douse the fire that burned within him. He flew between the trees, massive paws barely touching the ground as they drove him onward.

He found them there, secreted away between a copse of pine and mass of jumbled stone. With a mighty leap, he cleared a great boulder and landed in the middle of the man forms. He bared his fangs and growled at each and every one of them. When he locked eyed with Simmons, the guilt on his face was obvious.

He stood on his hind legs and towered over Simmons in his human form. Marcus dropped, his muzzle heading for Simmons neck and at the last instant, he clamped his fangs into the man's shoulder, letting his bodyweight drive the Were creature to the ground. Marcus bit hard enough to rip the skin, penetrate the muscle, and scrape the bone.

Simmons yelled in pain and immediately changed into his Werewolf form.

A challenge! Marcus only wanted to send a message to Simmons and the rest, but this was even better. A good fight would tamp the coals of his fury.

Simmons struggled beneath the great shaggy beast. Marcus let go when Simmons changed, but he hovered and once he stood astride the Werewolf, he attacked with renewed vigor, biting into Simmons' ear and shaking his head to rip a chunk of it free.

Simmons kicked furiously as he sought purchase from beneath the pack's alpha. The fire from Marcus' bite burned his entire head, but he continued to twist until he got his back legs beneath him and pushed for all he was worth.

Marcus rolled away with a piece of Simmons' ear in his

mouth. He spit it away, and they started to circle each other, but only briefly. Marcus was bigger and used his size to his advantage. He bull-rushed the smaller Werewolf, driving him toward the rocks. At the last instant, Simmons vaulted straight in the air and kicked off the rock face behind him, launching himself over Marcus' head. Simmons twisted as he passed and caught the bigger Werewolf's tail in his mouth.

When he hit the ground, he hauled backwards, trying to throw Marcus off balance. The bigger beast was more agile than Simmons gave him credit for. He twisted his body around and with tail in his mouth, Simmons couldn't react fast enough as Marcus' jaws slid past his muzzle and took hold of Simmons' neck.

It was all over except for the thrashing. As Marcus' fangs dug deep into Simmons' throat, he had not yet decided whether to let him live or not. As the smaller Werewolf flopped and went limp, completely surrendering to his fate, Marcus let him go. Simmons lay on the ground, whimpering. He changed back to human form and once the others received Marcus' approval, they moved him to a spot where he could sit and start to heal himself. They'd been eating well recently, so Simmons had the energy. All he needed was time.

"So, you bitches thought you'd plot behind my back. Well, fuck you. And you, and you, too," he told them from his human form. He stood naked before them all, his clothes outside the cabin where he'd left them when he last transformed. And he didn't care. He had to make a statement. There could only be one alpha, and that was Marcus.

"Your bullshit ends right here. If I say we move a thousand miles, we move a thousand miles. If I say you hunt and bring food back to the cabins, you do that. Do you limp dicks understand that? You'll eat what I tell you to eat, and you'll do what I tell you to do. Go get an elk and bring it back. I'm hungry. Now get the fuck out of my sight," Marcus commanded as he turned and walked back toward the cabin. It would be a long walk in his human form, but he was satisfied with the outcome and no longer twisted with rage. He'd stroll and think about what the pack needed to do next.

❖ ❖ ❖

Felicity smiled adoringly at each farmer, hanging from Billy's arm as they traveled from one greenhouse to the next. Billy had his speech set and he even smiled. It grated on his soul.

At first, but then he realized that the victories from confrontation that had been fuel for so many years held no such thrill for him anymore. Confrontation just made him angry. All he wanted was the people to do what they were supposed to do. Many had chosen their own professions, but others had been forced into their jobs, like the idiots he had keeping the people in line.

He wondered if that Walton guy would make good on his promises. The hunter. If he could find him, that would be a good first step. It'd be nice to have someone intelligent to talk with. He'd had too many lackeys over the years, telling him what he wanted to hear, then groveling when things went bad. Felicity showed him that it was better to hear the truth. At least that way he could fix it before it broke, before it could no longer be repaired.

So he smiled and thanked the farmers, then started asking them if there was anything they needed, noticing that there seemed to be more work than they could do. Like a miracle, Mark and Devlin showed up and did just that. They offered their services to the farmers and their greenhouse.

The famers looked at Billy Spires with reverence.

Billy always did what he said he'd do, but usually that was because of threats. More benevolent and less dictator. It made him feel funny, but in a good way.

When they were outside, Felicity pulled him close to her. "Why, Billy dear, I do believe you've turned over a new leaf. I'm not sure I've ever seen you act more natural. Shave off that tough guy exterior and we have a big, helpful, teddy bear. I think you are going to be surprised with what these people provide when they are working for you instead of working in fear."

Billy smacked his lips, imagining the taste a fresh tomato, eating it like an apple, with a little salt. It had been a while since they'd willingly shared the best of their harvest.

"Weekly trips, to gauge progress of course, and help them as we can," Billy said, looking into the distance. The wind rustled his hair as he squinted under the noon sun. He let his hand drift down Felicity's back and he cupped her butt. Could he be in charge without using a hammer?

The concept was foreign to him, but he was seeing it start to work. He was able to manipulate the people in a way where they liked it. He'd keep his eye on things, but hoped the approach would work. He didn't think his new security chief would beat people into submission if Billy ordered such a thing.

He stood there thinking and Felicity let him, watching him closely to see his mind work.

It was the first big step in a long line of steps that would ultimately lead to her riding in a vehicle. She really hated walking everywhere, but then again, that kept her shapely, which was what put her in this position in the first place.

❖ ❖ ❖

Terry climbed higher and higher, until he thought he'd breached ten thousand feet. He followed the hunter's tracks easily until the other man had found deer tracks. Then the horse was tied to a tree, where it must have freed itself since and run off.

The hunter had stalked more warily, but Terry still found his trail easy to follow. He saw where the man stopped and waited, then rushed off. Terry looked around the site carefully, watching for any movement, even though if the Weres showed up, he was screwed.

He stalked soundlessly, trying not to spook any wildlife. He felt like he was close and saw a scrape on a tree's bark up ahead. He saw the spent casing, picked it up, and pocketed it. The hunter had run from the spot, but soon stopped, took a knee and fired again. Terry recovered that casing, too. There were drops of blood not far off. The hunter's bullet had flown true and hit whatever was chasing him.

He smelled the body before he saw what was left of it.

Terry got past the site of what had been a frenzied, animalistic attack that had torn the man apart. But they'd left the rifle and ammunition. Terry knew that Weres didn't eat humans, which made this bunch ten times more dangerous. They were different and not in a good way.

"Fuck," Terry whispered as he dug through what was left of the clothes to recover unspent ammunition to go with the rifle. The man even had a small cleaning kit with him, which Terry appreciated, thanking the corpse for being a professional, then Terry bolted, moving as quickly as he dared to escape the kill site and the territory of the killer Weres.

He left the horse on its own, wishing it well in its freedom as he fled the area.

❖ ❖ ❖

"I sense someone," Adams said, but he was helping to half-carry Simmons. "Maybe we should check it out?"

The other two had gone off in search of elk, but they were heading higher up the mountain, away from the intruder. Simmons' head lolled as he continued to trudge doggedly forward, leaning heavily on his friend, back toward their compound. "I'm in no shape to go after anyone and if you go, I don't think I can make it back on my own," Simmons mumbled.

"There's something different about this one, I think. Ahh, there, he is retreating fast. Maybe we should broaden our reach, keep the humans from coming up here in the first place, but I don't want to bring it up if Marcus didn't sense him. Maybe we'll offer it as a hypothetical," Adams posed his random thoughts. Then he shrugged and continued dragging Simmons toward the cabins.

◈ ◈ ◈

Terry cleared the hilltop and headed downward, flexing his knees to absorb the shock of running downhill. He ran faster and faster as the slope lessened.

Only Weres and Vampires made him afraid. They had power that he could barely comprehend. Distance was his friend and he ate up as much of it as he could. At least he had a rifle, but it hadn't helped the hapless hunter. Still, he felt more comfortable carrying it. An AK-47, 5.56mm, but necked so it could take U.S.-standard 5.56mm ammunition along with its own, which did not fit into a NATO weapon. Had there been a ground war between the U.S. and Russia, that little advantage may have made a difference, but it didn't because neither country existed anymore.

Once Terry hit the end of the road, he slowed, then dodged behind a wall and double-checked his rifle as he watched the hills behind him, waiting patiently to see if anything followed. After an hour, he was convinced that he'd left the hills alone. He slung the rifle and marched off smartly, covering the distance quickly with ground-eating strides.

He checked the position of the sun. "Damn! I might get home in time for some of Margie Rose's fine cooking." He looked around. "Shouldn't come home empty-handed," Terry said out loud. He looked at the rifle, decided now was as good a time as any to try it out, then turned south and ran hard, to get out of town and closer to a forested area that lay to the south.

Once there, he stopped and watched, checking the sun again. He might not make it in time, but expected Margie Rose would make something, especially if he brought home fresh game.

He waited, patiently. A movement. *There!*

A spike buck rubbing his young horns against the bark of a tree. Terry estimated the distance at three hundred yards, a perfect distance for iron sights. He aimed just behind the shoulder and gently squeezed the trigger. The rifle kicked lightly, blocking his vision of when the round hit home, but the deer jumped forward, head first into the tree, and struggled to get free.

Terry saw the spot below the spine. High and to the right. He aimed quickly in front of and below the shoulder then pulled the trigger a second time. The spike buck collapsed in place. Terry looked left and right, making sure the sound of his rifle hadn't drawn unwanted attention. As he thought about it, he didn't know why it would, but that was his Marine training and not his current situation. Wild animals would run from a rifle's retort, not toward it.

He got up and jogged to his kill. A decent sized animal, he guessed it would be around one hundred pounds dressed. He strapped his rifle crossways over his back and pulled his knife to gut the buck and clean it enough to be carried to the house, maybe five miles away.

This has been a good damn day, he thought. He'd covered probably twenty-five miles and barely felt tired. He chalked it up to a good breakfast and his special physique. He and Margie Rose would eat well over the next few weeks. Terry also committed to taking some to Billy Spires, along with returning the rifle and the ammunition. He'd like to keep it, but a deal was a deal.

He started whistling as he methodically butchered the deer, caressing the soft hide, knowing that with a little time and some attention, he could tan it and make a nice shirt, maybe even a new pair of pants. He had no one to impress, he just wanted to be comfortable. His current gear was clean, but he'd had about enough of it.

After making quick work of the buck, he threw the headless carcass over his shoulders and started walking. Next stop, some of Margie Rose's fine cooking.

CHAPTER SIX

Billy Spires wasn't happy that his hunter had been killed, but his anger was offset by the return of the rifle and most of the ammunition. Five precious cartridges had been expended and although four casings had been returned, there wasn't much they could do with them.

Terry looked on expectantly. Billy looked back. Finally, Felicity harrumphed. "Maybe you two can just arm-wrestle and get it over with, but I don't want you boys fighting over me," she drawled and batted her eyelashes. Terry snickered, appreciating the interruption in the stare-down.

"Can I take that with me?" Terry asked Billy. The smaller man pursed his lips and thought about it.

"No," he said dismissively, gauging Terry's reaction. All the larger man did was lean back and cross his arms. They were both sitting at the table, mirroring each other's pose. Felicity shook her head.

"But you can take one of the old M4s. There's less ammunition for those, so we'll issue you ten rounds. Take it or leave it," Billy said with a smile. He'd spent his life lording his power over others and that wouldn't change overnight, but he was getting less pleasure from the dance.

Terry sucked on his tongue and bit the inside of his cheek as he looked at the ceiling. Of course he was going to take the M-4 carbine, but he didn't want to give Billy the satisfaction of answering too quickly. He returned his gaze to Billy's face and started laughing.

"Yeah, I'll take it, but I need a pistol, too. Got a .45 back there?" Terry looked hopeful.

"We do, but only two rounds for it. I got a .38 special with twelve rounds. Choose wisely," Billy replied.

"The .45," Terry replied without hesitation. "History suggests that one well-aimed round from the big boy is worth more than six from the popgun. I'll just have to make sure I'm in a position where I can't miss."

"Why such love for a big, heavy pistol with only two shots?" Billy asked, curious.

"Marine Corps," Terry revealed. Billy had never met a Marine before. He'd been told stories, most of which he never believed. No one could be that much larger than life.

But then he met Terry Henry Walton. "The hell you say. Where'd you serve?" Billy pried.

"Even if I told you, none of that would matter. Do you know where we conducted operations? What were you when the world fell, fifteen?"

"I was eighteen, but I guess I've aged well." Billy smiled. "And no, I wouldn't know if you were lying to me or not. You disarmed my guard without a problem and you tamed my enforcement team barehanded. And you've returned both rifles to me. You have a strange code of honor, Mr. Terry Henry Walton, that I haven't seen, so yeah, you're different. I'll believe that you were a Marine, but you work for me now. And I think you should probably call me 'sir,'" Billy sneered, reverting for a moment of guilty pleasure.

"I don't fucking think so. Let's go grab those thundersticks and I'll be on my way. I've got a security force to train and feed, which means we'll be working in the greenhouses, helping out the good farmers who grow stuff because we can't."

Terry nodded politely, first to the self-proclaimed mayor and second to Felicity. Billy wanted to be offended, but his jibe had fallen flat and been dismissed out of hand. The rest of what Terry said made sense. The security force needed help.

"Okay, let's load you up. Wait here, I'll be right back." Billy's hand lingered on Felicity's body as he stood, casually and deliberately rubbing his body on hers as he passed. With a final look at Terry, he walked out a back door.

Felicity made a beeline for Terry Henry Walton. He jumped from his chair and moved the other way around the table, keeping it between them as he looked at her through narrowed eyes.

"Why are you running away from little old me?" she drawled. Terry did not dignify her taunt with a response. "Big, tough Marine afraid?" She leaned over the table, letting her shirt droop to give Terry a view of what was underneath.

"Because Billy needs to know that I'm not after you. I won't let you pit us against each other. I need him to manage the town and he needs me to make sure it stays managed. I've seen the look in your eyes. I know that you believe this town can vault out of the dark ages, if we provide the right support to our engineer and mechanic. Which reminds me, I need to meet those two as they are more important than you, me, or

Billy Spires. They will move us forward. All we have to do is create the conditions for them to be successful. I know you get that, the power behind the throne and all. But you've no power over me," Terry stated matter-of-factly, all business.

❖ ❖ ❖

Billy stood behind the door and listened, satisfied with what he heard. So he could trust that man and all it cost him to find out was something he was going to give anyway, a rifle and a pistol.

How could he have a security chief who wasn't armed?

Billy left the two to their verbal jousting while he headed for his ad hoc armory. It was a closet with a padlock. He dialed the combination, unhitched the lock, and opened the door. It was sparse, so much more sparse than twenty years ago. Then, it was packed full of rifles, pistols, and ammunition. Over the years, people left and didn't come back. People died and weapons were lost. Ammunition had been used and not replaced.

He dug out the carbine and set it aside, pulled open the lid on an ammo can, and whistled. There were four boxes left, eighty rounds. He took one magazine and a box of cartridges. He was feeling generous. The M1911 .45 caliber pistol was already loaded. He dropped the magazine and checked. Two rounds. He cycled the action to confirm there was nothing in the chamber. He re-inserted the magazine, sent the slide home, and shoved the pistol into his belt.

When he returned to his receiving room, he found Felicity sitting in his chair and Terry sitting opposite. Felicity was scowling, and that pleased Billy Spires. He laughed out loud as he deposited the weapons and ammunition on the table.

Terry looked at the full box of twenty rounds, realizing that he'd passed some sort of test.

After checking the magazine and chamber of the old M1911, he reseated the magazine and tucked the pistol into his belt. He did not put a round in the chamber on purpose. When he was in the Corps, a lance corporal in the next barracks over was screwing around and shot his own pecker off. Although Terry had always been careful, he was extra careful after that.

He performed the same function check on the M4, before loading ten rounds into the old magazine and seating it. He slung the rifle over his shoulder, knowing that he would make a new sling, probably out of deer hide, so he could carry the rifle in a combat ready position instead of behind his shoulder where it was useless for rapid action.

"Thank you, Billy Spires. I think I'll have something for you in about a week as to a way ahead, triple production, improve power distro, and most importantly, increase population. I've been out in the wasteland and there are people out there who should be in here."

Terry shook his head before Billy could argue. "And no, they won't come to take what you have. If given the opportunity and support, they'll provide more than they use. A net gain. Does that sound like something you'd be interested in, Mr. Mayor?" Terry said with a smile. Billy kept his face neutral.

Fuck yeah, he was very interested in that.

❖ ❖ ❖

Terry jogged eastward along what passed for the main road. It was in good shape because the horse and cart traffic wasn't heavy. The worst thing was the road apples, the horse drop-pings. Once Terry reached the first greenhouse, he had an idea.

He saw barley and wheat and from that, knew he could make beer. Why was there no beer?

He offered to help in the greenhouse, although he had limited time. He worked like a fiend for what he estimated was thirty minutes before moving on. Then he did the same thing with the next three greenhouses. They all invited him back whenever he could make it.

Terry was a hard worker, and he was building credit that he may or may not call in later, although his real reason was that he wanted to check up on his boys. He caught up with them in the fifth greenhouse. They were working, not as hard as they should have been, based on their actions as soon as they saw him. He waved to the farmers, greeted them warm-ly, then offered to help for a brief time before he needed to take his people out for security training.

When he joined Mark and Devlin in weeding and mov-ing detritus, he smiled kindly before he spoke. "It looked like you two were fucking off. Tell me I didn't see that."

Mark put a hand on Devlin's shoulder. "I could tell you that, but you saw what you saw. Sure, we could have been working harder, should have been working harder..." He hesitated as he was speaking, then shook his head. He had nothing else to say.

"Why don' they have any beer here?" Terry asked.

"What?" Mark asked, taken by surprise. He expected to get his daily comeuppance, but that wasn't it.

They continued to work, moving, lifting, cleaning. The farmers followed behind, watering and touching up the plants. They looked happy, which neither Mark nor Devlin could understand. Digging in the dirt all day wasn't their idea of fun.

Terry seemed to be enjoying himself, joking freely with those who ran the greenhouse. Mark kept looking at the rifle slung across Terry's back and the pistol wantonly stuffed into his pants. With weapons like that, Mark wouldn't have to be subservient to the big man. A plan started forming in his mind, but then he dismissed it. In no way would he ever be able to take those weapons from the security chief. Mark watched as the man moved easily and adjusted quickly to keep the rifle in place. The pistol always seemed to be within a hand's breadth of being pulled to action.

Mark had never seen a pure warrior before, but if he could have imagined one, Terry Henry Walton would be it.

"Teach me," Mark asked in a near whisper. "Teach me how to be a warrior." Devlin wondered what had come over Mark.

Terry looked over at Mark, skeptical.

He nodded and grabbed some weeds. "I intend to, and you know what? Real warriors don't slack off, ever. Head on a swivel, working as hard as you can, until you get to something new, then you do that as hard and as fast as you can. I'm not sure you have it in you. Maybe he does." Terry pointed at Devlin with an elbow as his hands were full of weeds.

"I might not, but I think I can prove you wrong," Mark said flatly, working with renewed vigor and outpacing his colleagues on the last of his row. When he finished, he looked for something else to do and ended up carrying buckets of water for the farmer's wife.

When Terry and Devlin finished their rows, they gave their kind regards to the good people running the greenhouse and headed outside.

"What gives?" Terry asked Mark as soon as they were in the waning sun. "You're a total fuck every minute of every day since we met, and now, you want to learn from me. Why? So you can find a weakness and someday beat the master at his own game? I don't trust you, Mark, and I'm not sure I ever will."

Mark pursed his lips. "I've earned that. But understand, we've been out here all day with these people, the second day in a row, and you know what we saw? Billy Spires being nice to them. Shaking their hands and thanking them for the work they do." He pointed around the area. "I've been here most of my damned life and I ain't never seen anything like that before. Billy rules with an iron fist. The only difference I see is you. That woman's been here for almost a year now, so it's not her. If you can change Billy like that in just a few days?" He paused, took a deep breath and let it out. "Hell, Mr. Walton, I have a lot to learn." Mark ended contritely, looking at the ground.

Terry was taken aback. A day prior, he was ready to punch the man in the head and as often as it took to beat sense into his thick skull. And here he was, a seemingly changed man.

Devlin puffed out his chest and stood tall. "Me, too. I want to know everything you know, move like you move, kick ass like you kick ass," he added.

Terry shook his head. The world was so fucked up. "All right, gentlemen, you think you want this? Remember when you're face down in the mud, crying, I never promised you a rose garden. The only thing I can guarantee is that you'll be in pain, but it'll be a good hurt. You'll sleep fast, then we'll do it all again. In between, we're going to work here in the greenhouses every day, because humility is an important lesson. Now, run home and get that house cleaned up. Fix that front door of yours, too. I'll see you first thing in the morning. When you hear me, you better jump from your racks and be ready to go. Do you understand me?" They both nodded.

Terry snarled at them. "You will answer, 'Yes, sir!' Now do you understand me?"

Two shouts of "Yes, sir!" rang out and the men bolted, sprinting away before settling into a quick jog. Terry figured they'd slow further before they got home, but as long as they fixed the door, he'd be happy. Terry would be there early, before daybreak, and there would be hell to pay if that task wasn't done.

Terry walked back into the greenhouse to see if he could get a couple fresh things to bring to Margie Rose. They happily gave him two small peppers and a flower. He knew she'd like that.

Terry whistled quietly, walking home wondering what Margie Rose was going to cook when he gave her the peppers.

And the flower.

CHAPTER SEVEN

Billy wandered outside, walking in the cool morning air. He'd taken to doing that more often nowadays, because he needed to think. Billy felt like he was caught in a whitewater stream heading toward the falls. No amount of flailing changed his course.

He kicked a rock in the small garden that Felicity maintained. It had a few vegetables, but was mostly herbs and flowers.

Not that he was fighting it very hard. He hoped that the current took him downstream to more fertile land and not to a waterfalls. There was nothing he could do about it in either case. It seemed that the more he let go, the harder people worked. He was seeing his little town become a place where people wanted to live, and not a place where they had to in order to survive.

He determined to go see his engineer and mechanic, see

what they had in the queue and he hated to say it, but see if they needed any help.

For the first time in his life, Billy saw people willing to work without having to apply the lash. He didn't know how long they would stay motivated, probably until the first crisis, he mused. If that happened, well, then he'd pull the whip back out and apply it liberally, just because they made him believe in the touchy-feely crap.

He chewed on the inside of his lip. "Felicity, what have you done to me? I'm pussy whipped, that's what I am." He kicked a rock, then a second. He snarled and went back inside, to his weapons locker, where he pulled out the AK-74. He noted that Terry had cleaned it before he returned it. It was ready to fire. He took two magazines and the rifle, walked back out the front door and headed for the hills. He needed to kill something, prove to himself that he still could.

❖ ❖ ❖

Five days had passed and Jim was able to finally join Mark and Devlin, which meant that he was going through the same modified boot camp that Terry was currently torturing the others with.

"Holy fuck!" Jim exclaimed as he fell on his face after what seemed like an infinite number of pushups.

"You know what you're made of, candy ass? You can't find out if you don't push yourself one step farther than you've ever gone before. That's when we all get to see the real you, big man," Terry hissed inches from the man's face. Jim's big cheeks turned red as he got mad, but Mark had told him this was what they were going to do, so he was playing along.

But damn!

He struggled through another five pushups.

Another hiss, "Look at that. You had a little left in the tank after all, didn't you, candy ass?" Terry taunted the big man constantly. He wanted to see him break.

Mark did what he was told without complaint. Still, Terry didn't trust him. No one changed their tune that quickly. Terry never let his weapons leave his body. He suspected Mark was biding his time until he could secure the pistol or rifle and then shoot Terry in the back from a safe distance.

Devlin was a completely different story. He was as motivated as any raw recruit that Terry had ever seen. He was internally driven and for the right reasons.

That was good because there weren't any rose gardens and if there were, they sure as hell wouldn't be given out.

Terry laughed at his own joke. None of these people would understand. They were too young to remember any of the best Marine Corps recruiting commercials. The good news with that was he could parrot the best lines and they would all be new to his new recruits.

These three also had the fear of death, something he didn't have when he was going through training all those years ago. He looked about fifteen years younger than he really was and felt even younger than that. The boost he'd gotten had made him stronger, faster, and age more slowly. He was finally putting his abilities to a use of which his benefactors would approve.

He stood back and watched as the men struggled to remain in the pushup position. "Get up," he growled. They climbed to their feet. The dust mixed with their sweat and had created mud tendrils tracing down their faces. They did him the courtesy of standing at attention.

While they stood, breathing heavily, Terry heard someone

lumbering up the road toward the home where Terry's security force lived. The hastily repaired door stood at its front and weeds filled a lush green yard. As long as the door worked, that was all Terry cared about. He turned and saw the fat man with the smashed face. Terry's butt-stroke had done a number on the man. When he arrived, he stopped in front of Terry and stood there, looking at the three men still breathing hard from their physical exertions. He was breathing hard from simply walking up the hill.

"What?" Terry asked, trying to be demeaning.

"Billy Spires told me to join you, get some training," he said weakly, still looking at the men as fresh beads of sweat appeared on their heads and arms.

"Hey, boys, I think I have a job for you. Why don't you take Smashmouth here for a little run. When you get back, we'll do some fire team immediate action drills, start learning how to attack in ways that will strike fear into your enemy's heart."

"But, but, but…" the man stammered. "My name is Ivan."

"GET. OUT. OF. MY. FACE!" Terry screamed. Mark, Jim, and Devlin ran past, grabbing Ivan's arms on their way. His feet barely touched the ground as they hauled him down the road. He complained and cried for as long as Terry could hear.

"What are you doing to me, Billy Spires?" Terry asked the sky. He watched as the four men stumbled away on the five-mile track that he had laid out for them.

It had only been a week. The men were still breaking down, but Terry would have to rush them into service. He needed more people, weapons, and ammunition if he was going to help Billy consolidate what was left of the great state of Colorado and start building a new infrastructure around his engineer and mechanic.

They needed talent and they needed workers.

So much to do, but that meant taking a force strong enough to protect itself to find the other communities and convince those people to give New Boulder a chance.

When would the timing be right for all that?

Maybe next year. In Terry's twenty years of self-imposed exile, he had learned patience. If it was next year, so be it. Having a stocked arsenal was probably the one thing that would provide him the greatest comfort. Once a Marine, always a Marine. He loved sending rounds downrange. It provided him a certain measure of peace.

He needed that as his past still haunted him. He saw his wife's face in his dreams. Only Margie Rose knew anything about him and she wouldn't tell.

❖ ❖ ❖

Marcus watched his pack as they crouched on a bluff overlooking the human settlement on the outskirts of what used to be Boulder. They could see activity, sense the warmth from the greenhouses, feel the power from the electrical generation system. Lights twinkled in one small area, then, a line of lamps lit up, illuminating a long expanse of road.

"Would you look at that? Our locals are starting to regain the past," Marcus stated.

The others nodded politely, not sure which direction the alpha was trying to take the conversation. No one wanted to be on the wrong end of a beat down. He'd gone to the extreme to reinforce his position. The other Werewolves were on the defensive, guarding their words and actions carefully.

They'd eaten the last of the elk they'd killed. The animals had moved to higher elevations to avoid as much of the day's heat as possible. Soon, Marcus would have to follow with the pack if elk were going to continue to be their staple.

"I think we need to take a closer look. Who wants to volunteer to go undercover into that town? The rest of the pack will follow the elk, but we'll be back in a few months. So that will be the job. Go, endear yourself, live among them, then we'll see what it all means come the fall." Marcus laughed when he saw everyone freeze.

Finally, his mate spoke up. "I'll do it," Charumati said. Marcus glared at her. She was a strikingly beautiful woman, as all Weres tended to be, but she was exceptional with eyes that bordered on purple, surrounded by thick and long eyelashes. Around her heart-shaped face, dark brown hair hung well below her shoulders. On one side of her head, a silver streak trailed down her hair. Brown with a silver streak was the true color of her pelt and she liked carrying it in human form as a badge of her Were honor. She was tall, almost six feet, with long legs making her shapely body that much more statuesque.

And she was his mate, but she was also one of his greatest enemies. At any moment, he expected they would fight one final battle from which the loser would not walk away. He wondered if she volunteered just to get away from him. He snarled, raising one side of his lip as he sneered at the others.

"What the fuck is wrong with you? Not a man among you? Sit there with your tails between your legs, you fuckwads?"

He turned towards her. "And you! Just go, you fucking bitch! Fuck off. All of you!" Marcus shouted as he threw an arm up, storming away.

Charumati raised one eyebrow and held her hands up innocently. "What? Did I do something wrong, pet?" she taunted, knowing that Marcus could hear her. He stopped for a moment and she crouched, thinking that the final fight had arrived. But it wasn't to be. He stripped while staring her in the face, bundled his clothes and changed into his Were form. Then, he left them and raced into the woods.

The chill in the air had nothing to do with the warm of the summer day.

Char shrugged, waved, and headed downhill with just the clothes on her back. She'd think of what to tell the townspeople during her stroll. She was in no rush. Maybe she'd fall a few times, look more convincing as a damsel in distress. Didn't everyone love one of those, rushing to their aid?

With that thought, she dove head first down a trail of rocks and rolled until she hit the bottom. "Ow!" she exclaimed, realizing that she probably could have waited until she was closer.

Her body would start to repair itself, but she'd walk with a limp for a while. Then she realized that if she took too long, she'd have to do that again because she'd be healed. But the blood stains on her clothes would be real. The weeds in her hair looked convincing. "Next time, maybe you think a little more before you act?" she cautioned herself.

"So where do we go from here?" Char asked no one as she continued walking downhill, starting a healthy conversation where she was the only one talking. She had spent too much time alone. Maybe the people would provide some entertainment, and it had to be better than the constant fights with Marcus. He'd grown so paranoid, she had no idea what he'd do next and that scared her. She didn't want any part of that.

Maybe she'd find a champion among the humans. *Wouldn't that be funny?* She laughed. She knew that she would be the most dangerous creature there and they wouldn't have a clue. The men would all vie for attention and maybe she'd give them just a taste, enough to build her own pack of potential suitors.

Just in case she needed them to do something for her.

❖ ❖ ❖

Billy congratulated the engineer and the mechanic on their accomplishment of extending the electrical grid. He hadn't realized how close they'd gotten, but when he showed up, they used the opportunity to showcase their work. Billy shook their hands and smiled, then realized what he was doing. He looked behind him to see if Felicity was there, continuing to manipulate him.

"Damn that woman!" he blurted. The engineer looked at him sideways.

"Excuse me?" the mechanic asked. Billy realized that he didn't know their names. He had always called them just engineer or just mechanic, but those titles had now become names of honor. They were the names they used when he wasn't around. He didn't understand that either. Maybe he'd been soft all along, only he didn't notice.

Nah, that couldn't be it. He was plenty tough.

"I'm going hunting. If I get anything, I'll make sure you get a healthy cut of it. Keep charging, gentlemen!" he said and nodded as he walked away. The two men beamed at their boss.

What the fuck have I become? he asked. Those were Terry Henry Walton's words, not his. *Goddammit!*

He headed west, reveling in the light of the lamps overhead. The grid was active. There was a separate power line to his house, but now, all the homes on this section of the grid would have power. That meant a couple old factories could be brought back to life, but what would it take to fire up the equipment, and what could they produce? What raw materials would they need?

People. He needed more people, a lot more people, to rebuild the infrastructure and then turn the town into a city.

After he finished hunting, he'd plan for a trip around the region, find more survivors and invite them to New Boulder, show them that technology and civilization was returning.

He needed to talk with Terry. If anyone could make that happen, it would be him. He also knew that it was dangerous in the wasteland. Who better than his security chief to accompany him?

Putting those thoughts behind him, he turned his nose toward the hills and sniffed the clean air of a non-industrialized world. Maybe that would change, maybe it wouldn't, but for now, it made for a good walk. He strode briskly away, heading for the road that would take him west into the hills.

❖ ❖ ❖

The runners returned after almost an hour. Mark, Devlin, and Jim were angry. Ivan was soaked in sweat and Jim was mostly carrying the overweight man, which completely befuddled Terry Henry. How could anyone get like that when food was so hard to come by? He shook it off. The man would trim weight rapidly as his calorie burn had just increased a hundredfold.

"Where do you live, Ivan?"

He pointed toward town, panting and unable to speak.

"WRONG!" Terry yelled, pointing to the house behind them. He had taken to calling it the barracks for lack of a better term. "In the barracks with you, Smashmouth." He nodded to his boys and they dragged the other man away.

"Mark, Devlin, come back here after you've tossed him into the tub," Terry called after them.

They returned barely twenty seconds later. From in the house, Ivan was yelling at how cold the water was. There was no pleasing some people.

"Can you two shoot?" Terry asked without preamble.

"I've never fired a gun," Devlin said, looking at the ground.

"That's good since we don't have any of those. We have a rifle and a pistol. Do you know about rifling?" Devlin shook his head.

"This is my rifle, this is my gun." Terry pointed first to the rifle over his shoulder and then to his groin. "One is for shooting, the other for fun. Nothing?" Both men shook their heads. At least they didn't have any bad habits.

"Well, gentlemen, we're going to learn how to shoot because our first big test is we're going after more rifles. We need to be the best armed of anyone we run across and that means more than just these. We need to train in how to shoot and move, cover each other as we attack, or build a withering wall of fire should we find ourselves in a defensive position. That is what made the Corps great. Combat turns boys and girls into warriors; training is the key to making that transition as painful as possible for our enemies. I know it's only been a week, but once you have your own weapons, I will need to trust that you won't shoot me. How can you prove to me that I can trust you?" Terry asked as he ended laying out his operational plan for the near term of his security force. His strategic plan looked much further out.

Mark shrugged. "I don't know, besides giving me a chance." He pointed. "Devlin can watch my back and if I do

anything, he can put one between my shoulder blades, because I'd deserve it. Trust isn't something you can just give
away freely. It has to be earned, and I'm doing what I can,
but only you can decide whether you trust me or not," Mark
admitted, not trying to convince Terry one way or another.

"Deal," Terry replied, holding out his hand. They shook
to solidify the agreement, then Terry took Devlin's hand as
well. "You have a key role here. You need to be ready at all
times to shoot him. Let me go talk with Billy Spires and see
what we can do to get some firepower." Before Terry took a
single step, he heard the report of a rifle, far in the distance. It
was distinct because there were no other sounds like it in this
post-apocalyptic world.

Terry's hearing was better than any human's, too. He
checked to see if the others had heard it and they had.

"A single shot, sounded like it could have been fired from
the AK. So, combat analysis, what do you think that was?"

Devlin scrunched his eyes as he was deep in thought.
Mark shook his head. "Billy must have gone hunting," he
said. Devlin nodded slowly.

"Perfect. You two help bring dickhead up to speed regarding the new rules that he gets to live under. Keep in mind,
that no matter how good a unit is, there's always a weak link.
Right now, it's him, but I expect he knows how to do things
that we'll need. When that happens, someone else becomes
the weak link. No matter what you do, someone will always
be that person. Keep that in mind as to why we won't simply
discount that man. He might figure it out, but if he always
fails to keep up? Then he doesn't meet the minimum stan-
dards to be a member of the FDG," Terry stated, adding a
new acronym.

No one questioned him as to what it meant. At some

point they would, when they felt like real members of the team.

"I'm going out there to help Billy carry his kill. We'll talk weapons and the way ahead. It doesn't get any better than that!" Terry turned and left without any delay.

❖ ❖ ❖

Billy was gutting the small doe he'd shot when he heard a noise. Thinking a bear had smelled the blood, he dove to the side, grabbing his rifle as he rolled to a kneeling position, ready to shoot.

A tall woman stood there with her hands up, watching him carefully. There was no fear in her eyes as Billy pointed his rifle at her. He dropped the barrel when he realized his AK was aimed at her. She was stunning. She was also a bit of a mess. Blood stained the tears in her clothing. Leaves and grass were trapped in her long brown hair. The silver streak drew his eye, but she was young, maybe in her early twenties, Billy guessed. He stood with his mouth open as he eyed the woman who put the gorgeous Felicity to shame.

"I'm sorry about that. You startled me," Billy apologized as he slung his rifle and approached her, offering his hand still covered in blood from when he was cleaning the deer. She took his hand in both of hers and raised it to her mouth. She licked his index finger clean, then bit her lip playfully as a small drip of blood ran toward her chin.

He jerked his hand back. "What the fuck was that?" he demanded.

"It's just a little deer blood. You eat what you have to in order to survive. I was on my own out there, for years, before I stumbled across this place, found you. I'm Charumati, but my friends call me Char. You'll call me Char, won't you?" she said. Billy couldn't tell if she had an accent or not.

"Sure, babe, I'll call you Char. Wait until Felicity gets a sight of you. There will be some hell to pay, and I think I'll be the one fronting the cash. Yeah, what are we going to do with you?" Billy asked, unsure of what the next few hours held. He was still put off by the blood licking, but not enough to change what he was thinking. Everyone had their idiosyncrasies.

Another sound, and Billy turned, but he didn't bring his rifle to bear.

Terry Henry Walton stood on the road and looked at the tall, young woman through narrowed eyes. He seemed frozen as he stared, but it wasn't with the look of a beauty-smitten man. It was one of the hunter as he faced a predator. Then the look vanished and Billy wondered what he'd seen.

"Good morning, ma'am," Terry said as he approached. "My name is Terry Henry Walton." He raised his hand to his brow, almost too quickly to see. Her hand shot up beside her face, ready to block the blow she thought was coming. Terry scratched his head, then lowered his hand slowly. Billy was watching them both, but missed the exchange.

Char was intrigued, but wary.

"Terry is my security chief," Billy interjected in a ham-handed way of establishing his authority.

"Yes, I am, and proudly so. Thanks, Billy. I heard your shot and thought I'd come give you hand carrying that beast back into town. So, let's take a look…" Terry pulled his knife when he saw that the cleaning had only just begun. He made quick work of it, keeping his eyes away from the Werewolf. He knew that she was watching him, trying to figure him out. He wouldn't give her the satisfaction.

MARTELLE and ANDERLE

What the hell are you doing here? he asked himself. *And where did you come from?* A bitch, all alone? There had to be more of them and that scared him, reminded him what he'd come for.

"Billy, another reason I came was I wanted to talk about weapons for my boys. I'll need some horses. We have a little ways to go, but I think we can find a stash of the good stuff. We'll talk more later." Terry had planted the seed and that was sufficient. He didn't need to reveal anything else to the Werewolf.

"We'll talk about that later, Terry. Can you carry that by yourself? I think the lady could use an arm." Billy Spires delivered his best smile, but he wasn't anything to look at. His only attractive quality was power, and that wasn't very much in the big scheme of life. It had worked before when he was the big fish in the small pond, but with Terry's arrival, he'd learned that he was a small fish in a small pond. It made him angry, but Terry hadn't betrayed him, not yet anyway, and he seemed to have no interest in the new woman.

Billy thought that Terry may have been gay. He didn't care, although he could trust a gay man around his women, and Billy already claimed the new one. Billy looked forward to watching the women fight over him. Maybe he'd end up with both of them tonight. That thought buoyed his spirits immeasurably.

Char took Billy's arm as they walked away. Terry threw the animal across his shoulders and shook his head. Billy had shot a young doe, barely bigger than a large dog. That was wasteful. Terry would let Billy know when they were alone. If he brought it up now, Billy would take it as an affront, posturing to demean the mayor in front of the new woman.

Terry watched them walk. Char was flirting just enough,

but not too much. Billy was taken, of course. They walked like that, Billy doing most of the talking, which was by design, because there was no way she could explain her presence to any rational human being. She showed up with nothing in the middle of nowhere, looking like she just walked out of a Hollywood makeup room.

Billy was smart, and Billy was an idiot.

Char continued to steal glances at Terry, the mystery man. She sensed something was different, but couldn't put her finger on it. She had time and she'd find out.

As they approached Billy's fairly large yet nondescript home, Terry started to giggle. He'd seen Felicity watching out the second floor window and the look on her face was priceless. She didn't let Terry down as she burst through the door into the front yard and intercepted the three as they approached.

"Who is this slut?" Felicity asked, her words razor-edged. Billy Spires looked to Char, then back to Felicity. Terry found somewhere else to look when Billy glanced his way.

"Why, Felicity dear," Billy attempted to drawl, mocking the woman who shared his bed. "This is Charumati, but we can call her Char." He smiled pleasantly. He thought he could smell Felicity's ire, which was bizarre as she usually smelled like some flavor of wildflower.

"Of course we can," Felicity said, standing on the sidewalk with her arms folded, blocking the way inside. She glared at Char. Terry wondered if the Werewolf was going to burst into flames from the intensity of the look.

"I'm no threat to you, Felicity," Char finally said. "I was lost in the woods and when I heard the gunshot, I knew that I'd finally found civilization. So here I am. I'm not horning in on your action, sweetie."

Terry couldn't stop watching. Billy was crushed. He wanted a cat fight.

"Let's not be hasty. We'll sleep on it and then see what the morning brings," Billy offered.

"I agree, Billy dear. She's not staying here. Period." Felicity remained rock steady, blocking the way to the door.

"We need to do something with this venison," Terry suggested, but no one moved.

"What about you, Terry? Do you have any extra room in your house?" Char asked without taking her eyes from Felicity.

"What?" he said, caught off guard.

"The nomad is just like you, showed up from the mountains, not that long ago. He lives with Margie Rose. Yes, I agree. You should stay there. For now," Billy added

"What?" Terry repeated. His eyes, for once, darting back and forth between Billy and Char, alarmed. The deer slung across his shoulders forgotten at the moment.

"That's settled then," Billy declared. "Bring that animal into the kitchen so we can prepare it. You take some with you, and I need to send some to the power plant for the engineer and the mechanic."

"What?" Terry said for the third time. Billy had just put a Werewolf in his home. His mind raced, trying to remember everything he knew about Werewolves which was summed up as...

They were dangerous.

Felicity walked coldly past Billy Spires, glaring at him along the way. She took Terry's arm and led him around the side of the house to the kitchen entrance. It wouldn't do to drip blood through the house. That wouldn't do at all.

CHAPTER EIGHT

Sawyer Brown looked at the rough men in his charge. He had twenty-three soldiers total, but for this, he was only going to take eight. Ever since he'd gotten word about a settlement to the north, he'd wanted to go there, but hadn't been able to before now. With the latest raid into Kansas, he'd discovered horses and brought them back to his enclave south of Denver.

Sawyer called himself General of the Army of the Rockies. He loved civil war history and considered the fall to be a second round in the north versus the south.

He never knew that the nukes that fell weren't from the United States and the destruction wasn't self-induced. He didn't care about any of that, because he was somebody, and had been ever since the fall.

Because the biggest and strongest survived. And that was him.

MARTELLE AND ANDERLE

Sawyer had been in his prime, a man twenty years old, when the end came. A construction worker since his early teens, he moved materials through brute force. At six and a half feet tall, he towered over his co-workers and after the fall, he towered over the other survivors. He took what he wanted, gathered minions to serve him, and turned them into the ultimate scavengers.

They were set to become the ultimate raiders, too. He was on his way to building an unstoppable army, but the more he wanted to project his power, the more he feared that people would take what he had gathered. That was why he decided to leave so many men behind.

He needed to protect his treasure, and that was how he thought of it.

In this new world, people like him had come out on top. Sawyer wasn't the man's real name. He liked the band and after the fall, names didn't mean anything anymore. His old persona disappeared and he became Sawyer Brown, a man larger than life.

"Get the fuck in here!" he yelled from the couch in the cabin he called home. He cared little about the fineries of society. Power didn't require them. Plus, it gave him a certain amount of pleasure to have his people wait outside. He'd call them on occasion to recognize that they existed, but they were all second class citizens. No one mattered but him.

Three men rolled through the door, trying to act cool in the rush to please their master.

"How are those saddles coming?" he demanded. The room smelled of sweat and it was dark, because Sawyer liked to keep his men at a disadvantage. They entered from the daylight and could barely see.

"Slower than we thought, boss, but we've got too many

lazy bastards around here," the first man said defensively, knowing how quickly pain would follow the delivery of bad news.

Sawyer slammed a meaty fist on his table and then used the same hand to point at them. "Well, get back out there and help! I want those saddles or you stupid fuckers will find yourselves riding bareback. You get me, dumbass?"

"Yes, sir!" the man declared and bolted from the cabin, followed closely by the other two.

"What do you think, Clyde?" Sawyer asked the mutt curled up on a blanket on the floor.

The dog didn't answer.

"I don't give a shit if they're uncomfortable riding bareback, but they won't be able to keep up and that matters. I guess we wait another day to go north, see what the good people near Boulder have to say about coming under our protection. Why haven't we found them before now, Clyde? Denver is still a little hot. Yeah. It's like a big, ruined moat. But the horses, Clyde, the horses will help us grow the empire! You don't like the horses, do you buddy?"

The dog snuffled, watching his master to see if a treat appeared. It didn't so the dog went back to sleep.

Sawyer leaned back in his chair, his hands together behind his head. "Wait until those stupid fuckers up there get a load of me!" He sneered, dreaming greedily of the plunder.

❖ ❖ ❖

"I'm home Margie Rose and—" Terry paused. "I have company," he finally finished. The older woman had been in the kitchen, evidenced by wiping her hands on her apron as she entered the living room.

"Oh my!" she exclaimed. "I think you are the most beautiful woman these old eyes have ever seen. And you, my beautiful man! What a wonderful couple you make."

"Whoa!" Terry belted out. Char stole a glance at Terry's face and giggled. She walked elegantly across the room and embraced Margie Rose.

"Is there any way I can stay here tonight? I've heard such wonderful things about you," Char purred. Margie looked at Terry, her eyes twinkling and a grin pulling at the corners of her mouth. Terry vigorously shook his head and pointed in the direction of the third bedroom. Margie Rose sighed, not yet giving up on her dreams of being a matchmaker.

"Let me show you to the spare room, dear. What should I call you?" she asked warmly.

"My name is Charumati. It's sanskrit and means intelligent, wise, and a beautiful lady. It is quite a mouthful and my parents blessed me with it. I've spent my whole life trying to live up to that ideal and I love it. My parents meant the world to me. Call me Char, and that's enough about me. Let's hear about you, Margie Rose. Tell me your story," Char implored, holding onto the older woman's arm.

Margie glowed and Terry shook his head, wondering what kind of chaos the Werewolf was going to create. What was her game? *Nothing good can come from this*, he told himself, mumbling aloud.

"Where are your things, dear?" Margie finally noticed that Char had nothing. The young woman held up her hands and shrugged.

"I was lost on the mountain and fell. This is all I have." she said, frowning dramatically.

Margie turned and pointed. "You march right back to those woods and find her stuff, mister!" she ordered. Terry looked from one face to another, while Char smiled at his confusion.

Maybe we can just ask her to turn into a Werewolf where she doesn't need any stuff, Terry thought. Before he could come up with a reply that he could actually say out loud, Char came to his rescue.

"There really is nothing. It's refreshing to start over. I'm handy with a needle and thread. Do you possibly have anything I might be able to work with?" she begged the old woman.

Terry was happy to see the two disappear into Margie Rose's bedroom. Margie was chattering the whole time.

The daughter you never had. Terry went to the kitchen and started slicing the shank of deer into steaks. He wondered how Werewolves liked their meat.

Raw?

Goddammit! How did I get stuck living with a fucking Werewolf! FUCK! he screamed internally.

If she discovered that he knew, his life would be forfeit. In a straight up fight, he was pitifully aware he couldn't beat a Werewolf. If he could bring his firepower to bear, that would even things up.

He could never be apart from his weapons, not that he was anyway, but even behind a locked door, he would have to sleep with the rifle at his side and his pistol under his pillow. *Maybe I'll move to the barracks, he thought, but I can't leave Margie Rose alone with her.*

Fuck!

Terry yelled a disjointed good-bye as he headed out the door, determined to go to the barracks after first stopping by to ask Billy about the weapons.

MARTELLE AND ANDERLE

❖ ❖ ❖

"Why in the hell did you bring that whore here? What the hell, Billy?" Felicity raged, stomping around the kitchen. Billy was butchering the deer and avoiding any part of this conversation. He expected to get a huge boost to his ego when he saw those two beauties fighting over him, but one had no interest at all and now all of the other's anger was focused solely on him.

She worked her way close to him, ignoring the fact that he was wielding a bloody knife. "Billy, you need to understand this about our relationship. It doesn't end because you think you've found another woman. It ends when I find someone else or you're dead," she said coldly, switching quickly to her warm southern drawl. "Is that clear enough, Billy dear? Maybe you can massage my feet later, but make no mistake, my lover, you are still in the doghouse."

Billy leaned over to kiss her forehead, but she walked away, swinging her hips to tease him. "Nice venison steaks for dinner and I'd like you to go with me when I take a bit to the engineer and the mechanic," Billy offered by way of asking, as a start to an uncomfortable truce.

He finished his work on the venison, putting most of it in their refrigerator, a benefit of being the mayor. He went looking for her, but she was nowhere to be found. He debated going without her and when he finally decided to leave, he smelled smoke. He went out back to find Felicity burning a pile of clothes.

His clothes.

"For Christ's sake, Felicity!" He watched the flames lick across the material, burning easily as it went. She didn't respond as she used an old shovel to stir the clothing within the fire, ensuring a complete burn. He sat down and waited. Leaving Felicity alone would probably not be in his best interest.

Terry didn't bother knocking when he saw the small tendril of smoke coming from the back of Billy's house. He ran around the corner and pulled up when he saw that it wasn't the house that was on fire. Billy looked at him and waved him over. Felicity smiled and continued to stir.

"Are those your..." Terry didn't need to elaborate.

"Yup." Billy watched stoically, not looking at his security chief.

Terry decided to dig right in. "I need rifles for my boys because I want to take them on a search and recovery for a stock of weapons and ammunition. There are a number of military bases around Colorado Springs. We'll go there and we'll find something. I know military, and I have no doubt that they hid bunkers of gear after the fall to keep the weapons out of the hands of looters. We just need to find them. We need weapons to find more weapons, because it's a dangerous world out there."

Billy didn't respond right away. "How many more people do you think are out there, Terry?" he finally asked.

Terry thought about that for a moment before answering, "I think there's more than we know. People like us—" He nodded to Billy. "—who survived it all and keep surviving. New families, strong men. I don't think anyone has power, though. We could grow, Billy. This small town can become a city," Terry suggested.

"My thoughts exactly. Horses?" Billy asked, watching his clothes go up in flames, Felicity moving one of the shirt's back into the fire.

"Five, for now, but Ivan might not cut the mustard. We

may have to kill him," Terry said matter-of-factly.

"I'd ask that you don't. Do what you can to get him to see the light. I'd hate to see my brother get himself killed."

Terry wondered if he meant a fraternity brother, brother-in-arms, or something like that. There was no resemblance at all. The two could not have been more different.

"I'll do what I can for him. Five horses then, and we'll train with them for a while before we head out. It'll probably take us a couple weeks to make the run, maybe longer."

Billy nodded slowly, stood, and waved for Terry to follow. Once inside, Billy opened the weapons closet and showed Terry everything he had. There were two more M16s, the older style. There were four total boxes of ammunition for them and a .38 with six cartridges in the cylinder and six more in a small bag. Billy offered it all. Terry took the two rifles, one box of ammunition, and the pistol. Billy put a hand protectively on the AK-74, which Terry had no designs on.

They went back outside where Felicity was finishing up. The flames were out as the ash pile continued to smolder, sending up great clouds of smoke. Felicity put the shovel aside and held her head high as she strutted past the two men, reeking of smoke.

"Let me freshen up, Billy dear, and then we can go," she said with a smile. Billy nodded briefly, his lips white from clenching his jaw. Terry looked closely at the smaller man, trying to come up with something to say.

"I got nothing, Billy," was what he finally settled on.

"Don't I know that," Billy replied. Terry snickered before he was able to stifle it with a cough, and excusing himself, he turned and walked away.

The barracks was less than a half-hour's walk from there. A walk he made briskly, trying to put as much distance between the new discordance of his adopted town.

He hoped that time would settle things down, and that the Werewolf would simply remain in human form. He didn't like hope as a plan. Actually, it made for a lousy plan, but none of that was within his control. The weapons he carried were.

His men would be armed with the best available. The ammunition for the rifles looked clean. The .38 shells looked sketchy. He'd give that to Jim. If the pistol blew up, he was most likely to survive, although the big man would probably forget that he carried the pistol, preferring a club instead.

Terry had been practicing with his bullwhip and found out that he liked it more and more. His heightened abilities made it possible to snap the whip as quickly as someone could draw a pistol. The tip of the whip easily exceeded the speed of sound, cracking through the air as it raced to its target.

Still, he had no intention of giving up his .45. He knew that he would always carry multiple weapons, because it was his way. One never discovered where the enemy was weakest until the last second, and at that point, there was no time to waste.

When Terry pulled the roughly repaired door aside, he found his boys eating dinner. Mrs. Grimes had just cuffed Ivan on the side of his head. He jumped up to threaten the old lady, but Jim grabbed him and bodily slammed him back into his chair.

Terry casually walked into the kitchen, around the table, and grabbed a handful of Ivan's hair, viciously yanking his head back. "Listen, Smashmouth, if you ever do that again to the good Mrs. Grimes, I will have to renege on my promise to Billy to keep you alive. Do you understand me? Keep in mind that just being alive doesn't mean pain-free. You shall suffer mightily. Now nod your head that you understand and finish your dinner. We have training in ten. No, make that five."

Terry pulled Mrs. Grimes into a hug and kissed her forehead. She slapped his knuckles with a wood spoon. Terry let her go. No one was safe around the gentle soul that was Mrs. Grimes. Maybe he'd take her with them instead of Ivan.

Or Char, just to keep an eye on their new resident Werewolf.

Once the men finished their dinner, Jim seized Ivan by the shoulders and dragged him from the house. He hadn't finished, but that was part of learning discipline. It was his first day, but Terry didn't cut him any slack. He made the four men sit down in a semicircle as he explained the M16 and its inner workings. He then covered, in nauseating detail, how to clean the rifle. Ivan grew bored quickly, so Terry took to kicking him in the leg every time his attention drifted.

He handed the rifles to the men and told them to disassemble them. After much yelling and prodding, both rifles were taken apart and put back together. It had been so long, and he had little patience for new recruit antics.

He told them to do it three more times, while he went back inside to see if Mrs. Grimes had anything left over, which she didn't but since Terry had arrived in town, her pantry had become well-stocked. She put together a quick salad using some of her homemade vinegar-based dressing, flavored with basil and rosemary.

It had some bite to it, and that made it all the more unique. Making vinegar is a drawn out and painful process. That made Mrs. Grimes a goddess in Terry's book.

She brought back a small, but significant piece of the old world.

He recommitted to brewing the town's first batch of beer to give them something else from the before time. Something that would make them crave more of civilization. Terry wasn't big on beer before the fall, but afterward, he craved it, almost embarrassingly so. Finally, he could do something about it.

The boys burst through the door to let him know they'd accomplished the task. They wondered when they'd be able to fire the rifles. Terry wasn't sure, but at a minimum, he required each of them to disassemble and reassemble the rifle in thirty seconds, then they could move to the next level of marksmanship training.

He watched each of them fumble through the rifle once more. When that was over, Terry judged he had enough daylight to make it back to Margie Rose's house. He gave the M16s to Mark and Devlin and the pistol to Jim, after making sure they were unloaded and no ammunition was available. Jim looked disappointed.

"You'll get your chance, big guy," Terry told him. "I don't ever want to see these weapons unsecured, do you get me?" They shouted in agreement, and he waved to them as he headed out, not looking forward to getting home and seeing what was waiting for him.

He didn't have long to wait. Halfway there, he could see the smoke from a fire, so he started running, then let his boosted body take over. When he sprinted into the yard, he found that Char had made a campfire and was burning wood. The venison steaks were on wood sticks that they'd just started roasting over the flames.

"I told you, Margie Rose. Men. All they think about is their stomachs, although that run was far more impressive than I would have ever imagined," Char laughed and Margie

Rose grabbed the young woman's arm and giggled.

"I thought the house was on fire," Terry said flatly, pulling up a log to sit on as he relieved Margie Rose of one of the steaks so he could cook it himself. He noted that Char was letting the flames lick her steak, but not enough to cook it. So she liked her meat rare.

Good to know.

CHAPTER NINE

The saddles are done, boss!" the biggest brown-nos-er's voice announced before the men even made it through the door.

"Saddle up, bitches!" Sawyer yelled as the door started to open, but the men never entered. They turned away and ran to do their boss's bidding.

Sawyer hitched up his pants, checked his pistols, two nine millimeters, one on each hip. He strutted out, his well-worn cowboy boots thumping on the planking. "C'mon, Clyde, we got work to do!"

Sawyer held the door as the dog ran out and onto the dirt path they called a street. The town looked like something out of the 1800s, a grouping of ramshackle buildings used in a variety of ways. Sawyer's home would have been the old jail. Maybe this had been the movie set for an old western. No one knew, and it didn't matter.

MARTELLE AND ANDERLE

Sawyer Brown thought it was perfect for his larger-than-life persona.

One of the early teenagers who aspired to be a lackey held Sawyer's horse while he took a couple steps and tried to vault to its back. Even with his size, he didn't get high enough. He slammed into the side of the horse, one shoulder bouncing off the hard seat of the saddle. He grabbed the pommel and pulled himself the rest of the way up, getting help from the young man. Sawyer kicked him away once he was up.

"Water?" he yelled. The eight other men held up a variety of canteens and metal containers. "No, dumbasses. Where's mine?" he corrected.

The young lackey ran off, quickly returning with an old gallon jug, three-fourths full. He presented the jug, at arm's length to stay out of range of Sawyer's kicking leg. The big man took the jug and shook his head. It would do. There were a lot of streams and in the world twenty years after the fall, pollution was at a minimum. They'd find more water than they could drink along the way. He angrily waved the young man away.

"Let's go, fuckers. East then north. Take the lead, Harold, you and Smeghead," Sawyer directed. He didn't know any of their real names. Whatever he called them when he first saw them was how they came to be known. And they didn't know his real name either, so that made it a fair trade, Sawyer thought.

❖ ❖ ❖

"Faster!" Terry yelled, exasperated at how Ivan held the others back. Jim and Devlin each grabbed an arm while Mark set the pace. Terry watched Mark closely, but hadn't seen any duplicity. Jim hadn't tried to attack anyone else, so Mark kept that part of the bargain, too.

Mark and Devlin carried the M16s. Jim had the .38 pistol tucked into a pouch that he carried. To Terry, it looked like an old fanny pack. He had to keep from laughing whenever he saw Jim wearing it.

Terry let the group pass him, then ran by, getting back in front where he set a blistering pace. Soon the group was far behind. Finally, they split up. Devlin bolted out front, then Jim. Mark hung back with Ivan for a little while before leaving him. Ivan stopped, bent over with his hands on his knees, and heaved.

When Devlin arrived, Terry put him in the front leaning rest, the pushup position. Then Jim and finally Mark. When he had all three of them, he tore into them.

"What the FUCK did you just do?" he screamed. No one answered. "You left a man behind, and that's something we never do. Do you get me?" A chorus of "yes, sirs" followed as they scrambled to their feet and sprinted back to Ivan. They berated the man and dragged him back to where Terry was standing with his hands on his hips. He wanted to send them into the mountains, feed them all to the Werewolves.

But that was a kneejerk reaction, fun, but wrong.

They stood at attention and waited as Terry paced back and forth, trying to think of what to do. He looked them over, one by one, and they avoided looking back at him.

"Bring it in," he told them in a low voice. The men broke their position of attention and stepped closer, but stayed out of arm's reach, wary about what would happen next. "This is called a teachable moment. I may have pitted you three against this man, in the hopes that he would come along faster than he has. But look at him. He ran until he puked, that means he pushed his body to the limit. Did any of you?" They shook their heads and looked at their feet.

"I was in the Marine Corps, a lifetime ago, and the worst thing you can possibly do is leave someone behind. We fight and we fight hard because we know we're not going to get abandoned. Our brothers are there for us."

Terry wanted the men to understand, take ownership for the success of their small unit. If he was going to grow this into a force that would bring and peace and stability throughout the area that used to be Colorado, he needed these men to believe and then sell it to the next bunch of recruits.

Pride was hard earned. And once they had it, they'd have to fight every day to *keep* it.

"Ivan, tell us, what are you good at?" Terry prodded, having not taken the time to talk with the man. Ivan shuffled his feet and shrugged. "Come on, there has to be something you do that others don't. Can you read?"

"I can read. It's what I do at night. I sleep better in the daytime," he said, barely above a whisper, as if embarrassed.

"Bingo!" Terry shouted. "Being able to stay awake through the night when all you're doing is standing watch is no easy feat, my man! We can use that unique ability of yours. I expect you can see well in the dark, too, since that's what your body is used to." Ivan nodded, lifting his head to meet Terry's sparkling eyes.

The larger man clapped Ivan on the shoulder.

"Nightwatch. Muscle. Speed. Smarts. Don't we have it all. This is what a team is all about. No one is great at everything. Know your strengths and don't let your weaknesses hold you back. That's what we are all about. Although I'm disappointed none of you asked what FDG stood for. Well,

I'll tell you. It stands for Force de Guerre and what do you think that might mean?"

Mark started to raise a hand, as did Ivan. Terry pointed to Ivan.

"Force of war," he stated.

"Why do you think I'd call it that, Mark?" Terry turned his attention to the oldest man of the group besides himself.

Mark pursed his lips and looked to the other men before speaking. "We take the battle to others. If someone wants war, let us bring it to them. New Boulder is a place where people need to not just feel safe, but *be* safe. That's our job. It's best if we protect them as far away from our town as possible. They don't need to know that we've fought our mutual enemies on their behalf. They need to go about their business, enjoy their lives. Then we come home and continue ours, just until the next time," Mark told the group.

Terry didn't immediately respond to that eloquent answer. It was exactly as he envisioned, the overarching reason that such a force should exist.

"FDG, gentlemen. Mark, you are, from this point forward, my corporal. The rest of you are privates. If we're going to be a real military unit, we need to be a real military unit. Do you get me?" he asked.

The men smiled and shouted a hearty "Oorah."

"And now we shoot, gentlemen. To the hills. I saw a cut that would make a good shooting range. You each get to take two shots. We will need to make them count. Follow me, for all you're worth, you useless maggots!" Terry took off running and the men cheered as they followed.

❖ ❖ ❖

Sawyer wasn't pleased. There was a lump in his saddle that didn't mesh with his backside. Every step the horse took exacerbated the pain, but he wouldn't show weakness in front of his men.

It didn't matter what he tried not to show, his constant squirming in the saddle told the men everything they needed to know. He would be surly and angry and take it out on them. They buried their heads and continued plodding forward, because at the end of the day, those on Sawyer Brown's side got to eat and got to sleep in relative peace. And those who weren't on his side? They died, hideously. The route took them some twenty miles to the east before they turned north on a back road through what used to be farm country.

Not long after they turned north, Sawyer called the group to a halt and sent four of the eight hunting. The other four set up camp. Sawyer walked around the area, trying to stretch out. He was miserable and found a variety of ways to take it out on his men.

They cowered as he approached. He hated it when they ran from a beating, which always made things worse. *Everyone gets their turn in the barrel*, he thought. *It makes them tougher.*

Sawyer heard the sound of the 12-gauge shotgun, once, twice. He hoped that meant two kills and not one miss. His man Stonehands was a good shot, and that was why he carried the scattergun. Birds and small game were plentiful in the overgrown fields. They'd found a big stock of the shells and had been milking them for the past ten years. Sawyer didn't know what they had left, but he expected his men to tell him if they were running low. The big man smiled, thinking that it was his genius that made everything possible. From weapons to horses to men. He had been lucky, but since he didn't believe in luck, he reasoned that it was because he was good.

When the hunting parties returned, one had a small deer, while Stonehands had three rabbits on the ground by the quickly-dug fire pit. "A new record, boss! Three with two shots," the man said proudly.

"Well, I'll be, Stoner. Next up is four, huh?" he said plainly, not getting caught up in the man's excitement. Sawyer waved them away to clean their kills elsewhere. "Hey! I didn't hear your shot. How did you get that buck?"

"He was caught up in a bush. Smeghead held him while I cut its throat," the man said, showing his knife.

"Good thinking, now get the fuck away from me," Sawyer Brown growled, feeling the pain from standing in one place too long. He sat down, but that hurt far too much, so he laid by the fire, resting his head on his backpack.

As he was falling asleep, he heard the men yelling at Clyde to stay back as the dog barked, hoping for something to fall his way. It was soon quiet, and Sawyer thought of the dog muzzle deep in a pile of deer guts. Venison sounded good. He'd wake up when it was ready. Serving him was his men's reason to live. If it wasn't, that was why he slept with his pistols and one eye open, Clyde by his side. He drifted, fighting it until the dog returned. When Clyde laid against his side, Sawyer Brown fell soundly asleep.

❖ ❖ ❖

The four men waited patiently while Terry watched them. Finally, Devlin held out a hand, palm up as if Terry was supposed to give him something.

"What? We're going to shoot, but when you finally pull the trigger on a live round, you are going to be so comfortable with your rifle that it won't scare you. We dry fire for two days before we finally pull the trigger for real. Then we take another day fixing whatever the hell you did wrong. If I feel it's fixed, then we send our second bullet downrange. Is that clear, gentlemen?"

They nodded. Terry set up the range, estimating a distance of one hundred yards where he put four targets of various sizes. He returned to the men and sat them down. He went step-by-step through the Marine Corps marksmanship training program. Of course, he had it memorized, because he had read it, from cover to cover and that was how his memory worked. He even knew the date he read it, but dates didn't matter anymore, only daylight and seasons.

They learned about sight alignment and sight picture. They each took turns squinting through the sights of the M16. A peephole in the back that they looked through, focusing their vision on the front sight post, then centering that in the middle of the rear circle and setting the focused front sight post in the middle of their target. Terry shook his head as he watched Ivan's contortions. He was right-handed but left-eye dominant, so he fought to get his face over the black stock of the rifle so he could focus with his good eye.

"Give the rifle back, Nightwatch," Terry said, giving the man a nickname with less baggage than Ivan or Smashmouth. "Here." He dropped the magazine and ejected the round from the chamber, then handed Ivan his .45, but told him he wouldn't be shooting it, not unless they found more ammunition. Terry would let him fire one shot from the .38 as a consolation prize.

They continued training with both the pistol and the rifle until they could no longer focus. They'd been contorted into various firing positions for most of the day. Terry told them to stand and shake things out. Then, he ran them through a long series of calisthenics to help them stretch. Terry ended by running them the five miles to the first greenhouse. He deposited Devlin first, then Ivan, then Jim, dropped Mark off, then ran to the last greenhouse. He had a promise to keep to the good people who supplied the food. He'd told them they would help and that was exactly what he made his boys do.

Work in the hope that the farmers could part with some of their crop that the men could take back to the barracks for Mrs. Grimes.

Which reminded him, Terry thought he'd have to go hunting again, since the venison was disappearing quickly with a Werewolf in Margie Rose's house. He avoided that place as much as possible, even though Margie Rose and Char were getting along famously. He needed to get some venison to Mrs. Grimes and the barracks, too.

Margie Rose was starting to get angry with him for his extended absences. Terry suspected that she was upset that her matchmaking was bearing no fruit.

He hoped an armload of fresh vegetables would placate her.

So he put himself to work along with his people. They worked for a solid hour and then he went back one by one to collect them. Each came out carrying their prizes, rewards for their continued work. The greenhouses were starting to deliver and the last few weeks of help took the edge off for the farmers. They'd developed the crops and nurtured them over the years, but finally, things were shaping up as they'd hoped. The men worked the greenhouses and in the surrounding fields where much was transplanted.

Next to the greenhouse that Terry chose was a healthy-sized field of barley and wheat. The farmers had planted it with the help of their cart horse and then did little with it besides getting rid of the weeds between the rows. Terry looked at the barley hungrily and was devising a plan to turn it into beer. He was still working on the farmers who didn't want to part with too much of their precious grain. They wanted it all for bread.

Terry wanted it for liquid bread.

He expected that they would compromise and that was why he always worked at their greenhouse, building credits to call in with the fall harvest.

Terry had fans. The farmers across the board were more than pleased with the help he provided and the change that had come across Billy Spires.

Terry always smiled and more importantly, although he wasn't a farmer, he seemed to be able to answer any of their questions regarding the history of the crops and optimal fertilization techniques. He had read a couple books on the processes way back when.

He recalled the charts that said when to add nitrogen, a little lime, or even horse manure. No one element was the golden egg. It was the balance that mattered.

The farmers were seeing more of their crops turning green and less dying. Terry was in good standing and he hoped to barter that for the opportunity to turn barley and wheat into mash as the first stage in brewing beer. He didn't have hops and that wasn't a bar to brewing. He accepted that his first stuff might not be great, but decided it would be the best that the world had to offer.

He was good with that.

In his head, he built a list of materials that he'd need for the brewing process, a large copper pot for boiling the wort and sparge water, those liquids that contained the sugars that would create the beer and then give it the alcoholic kick, a couple other vats for fermenting, some tubing, a screen for filtering out the hard bits, and then bottles to bottle the brew. He wondered if he could cap it or if he'd have to fashion soft wood into corks.

So much to do, but even a bad beer was better than no beer.

When he arrived at the house with his armload of vegetables, Char was waiting. She'd been lounging on the porch in a chair that had appeared during one of his absences. The Werewolf made a beeline for him, intercepting him while he was still in the street.

"What gives, big man?" She smiled, turning her head away just enough to highlight her perfect profile.

Let the flirt games begin, he thought, but he wasn't a player. "What do you mean?" he asked, knowing full well what she meant.

"It's like you're deliberately avoiding me. You eat, do the dishes, and rush to your room, locking the door behind you. I'm not a stranger, anymore, am I, TH? Can't we be friends?" she asked, tracing a single finger down his bare arm, then sliding it back up until she tickled the inside of his elbow.

He bristled at her use of TH. He reserved that for his friends and that was Margie Rose, who never used it.

Could it be that his only friend in this place was the Werewolf?

"Hell no," he mumbled.

"I'm sorry, TH, I didn't quite catch that," she said, looking at him through narrowed eyes.

"I'm sorry, I said, let's go. Let's get these vegetables inside where Margie Rose can work her magic. I forget, is it my turn to cook tonight?" he asked, trying to divert her efforts at being his friend to matters of a more non-contentious nature.

She walked at his side, holding his arm as if he were her escort. He probably could have carried the vegetables in one arm, but chose to use both so she couldn't find an excuse to hold his hand. She could probably smell his discomfort, the canine part of her reveling in the odd flavors coming from him.

She had to know that none of it was sexual attraction, which probably accounted for why she was trying so hard.

It was a game to her. As he was getting ready to bark at her to give him some room, Margie Rose appeared in the doorway with the kindest of smiles from the gentlest of souls.

How could he act angry in front of the old lady? He gave her his most winning smile.

"Margie Rose! What a sight to come home to. Look at what I've brought the lovely lady of this house." She opened the door to let him in. He walked deliberately straight to the kitchen, so he could start preparing dinner. Margie Rose followed him in and then shooed him away. He tried to resist, but she was adamant.

Then he had a thought, probably not a good one, but it was all he had.

"Do you fight?" he asked Char. She looked at him oddly, all pretense of the game gone from her face.

"What do you mean?" she answered with her own question.

"Sparring, hand-to-hand, self-defense? As I take the boys out, I need to know that the people here can protect themselves and that means you. Margie Rose doesn't have a single hostile bone in her body, but I have a feeling that you might have a few moves. Shall we?" He pointed to the door. She suggested he go first. He did, but sideways so he could keep his eye on her.

When they got into the yard, he unloaded the pistol and rifle and put them and all his gear to the side. He was loose from his walk, but stretched and flexed. She stood there, watching him disinterestedly.

He assumed his fighting stance, balls of his feet, knees flexed, left foot slightly forward, hands up but loose. He waved Char to him. At that moment, Margie Rose beat furiously on the window with a wooden spoon, wondering what was going on. When he took his eyes from Char, she struck. He caught a glimpse of an unnaturally fast fist coming toward his head in time to deflect some of the blow, but not enough to keep her from bowling him over.

It felt like his head had been hit by a freight train. He didn't remember falling, but when his back hit the ground, he continued rolling backward, throwing his feet up over his head until they hit the ground and he was kneeling. He put his hands up, expecting a follow up attack.

Margie continue to pound on the window, but Terry ignored it. This had become deadly serious.

"I knew you had it in you, but you know what they say…" He stood up slowly, his head pounding, but his vision cleared and he was ready to resume the fight.

"No, TH, what do they say?" she asked sarcastically, hand on hip.

"You can't keep a good man down," he laughed. He moved toward her with short quick steps, one foot forward and then the other, never crossing his legs or feet, always keeping his body squared up to hers. She stood with her arms at her side, unconcerned. He moved within arm's reach, yet she remained still. He jabbed at her face, not to hit, but to gauge her reaction. Her hands flew up to block the punch, then reached to grab his wrist, but he was already pulling it back as the real attack, the body blow, found its mark just above her waist.

As that punch landed, he dodged to the side. Her abdomen was almost as hard as a rock, like punching the flank on a horse. She darted forward into the space where he'd been. He let her get even as he followed with his left hand to the side of her head.

A blow that would have felled any of his men barely phased her. She turned and snarled as he danced backward, his face fixed as he looked for her next weakness. She'd been counting on her Werewolf speed to stop any of his attacks, but misjudged how fast he truly was.

She threw a handful of dirt toward his face but he dodged. She jumped high into the air and spun. She'd predicted his move, and the roundhouse almost hit home, but his hands were already up. He deflected her foot, guiding it past his head as he danced away, then resumed the attack. Margie Rose stopped pounding.

Only the two of them remained. Nothing else mattered. Char was focused like a laser beam on the surprising human. He'd caught her unaware once. There wouldn't be a second time. She danced forward, left, right, left as she approached, keeping him centered in front of her.

Her hands were raised, and she was ready to deliver the beat down the arrogant human deserved. *How dare you lay a hand on me, asswipe!* she thought as she snarled, as the Werewolf part of her threatened to overwhelm her being.

She was faster and stronger than Terry, but she was inexperienced in hand-to-hand combat.

When Terry dropped his right hand as if readying a haymaker, she darted through the opening, going after his exposed face to claw the flesh from his skull.

With an open-handed grab, he had her arm and then he turned, too fast for the eye to follow, pulling her through her own punch to drag her off balance. He used her speed and strength against her as he hip-checked her on the way past, driving her feet off the ground. He continued pulling with his right hand, around and down toward the ground. He kept his head tucked in in case she clawed at him with her free hand, but once off-balance, she simply flailed.

He slammed her into the ground hard enough that if she had been human, she would have broken most of the bones in her back.

As it was, she lay stunned for a few moments. Margie Rose came running out in a huff, smacking Terry on the head with her wooden spoon as she ran past.

"Ow!" he exclaimed, both in surprise and pain. He'd just bested a Werewolf in hand-to-hand combat and then got schooled by an old woman with a wooden spoon.

Char jumped to her feet, fire in her eyes. Margie Rose slid as she tried to stop and fell against the young woman. She bounced off as if she'd run into a wall. Char closed her eyes and exhaled slowly. When she opened her eyes again, all anger gone from her face. She looked at Margie Rose and smiled. "You worried about me, Margie Rose? Don't be." She pointed to Terry. "That wasn't anything. We were just playing."

"Holy cow! Oh my God! He slammed you into the ground. Terry Henry Walton! I never took you for such a brute. March right into that house, mister, and you finish dinner. I have to make sure you didn't hurt her!" Margie Rose snapped at him.

Terry held his hands up defensively, unsure of what to

say, but as before, Char came to his rescue.

"That's not necessary, Margie Rose. Terry was teaching me a valuable lesson. I was a little big for my breeches, and you know what, I think I am much more in tune with myself now. Why don't you take care of dinner, I need to thank Mr. Walton for the lesson." She patted the older woman on the back as she headed toward the house, scowling darkly at Terry.

He mouthed "what" at her and she pointed her spoon at him. He wanted to laugh, but wasn't sure what Charumati had in mind for him. He stepped back defensively, remaining on the balls of his feet as the Werewolf sauntered toward him.

"Nicely done, Mr. Walton," she said. "I concede. I believe there is much you can teach me and would like to begin training as soon as possible. Could I join your security force, please, or is that a boys-only club?"

His intent was to gauge her fighting skills, maybe smack her around a little to show he wasn't prey. He didn't expect to gain another recruit. If she practiced hand-to-hand with any of the others, she would probably kill them.

The little bit that Terry had taught those guys would not gain any of the men one extra second of life against the Werewolf. Which meant that next to him, she was the deadliest creature in town.

He shook his head. "God dammit."

Char smirked and Margie Rose beat on the window with her spoon, waving them into the house. Char looked towards the house. "She's going to break that window one of these days…"

CHAPTER TEN

Sawyer was as miserable as he expected to be. His seat felt like the soft spot in an old pumpkin, ready to give way at any moment. He finally stopped, got off the horse, and beat relentlessly on the lump with the butt of his pistol. When he climbed back onto the frightened animal, the lump was leveled, but he was still in pain. The others watched without amusement. He wondered...

"Which one of you fucks gave me the lumpy saddle? Come on, don't be a pussy. One of you did it on purpose. I better not find out or there will be hell to pay. I bet it was that little fucker back at the ranch who gave me a half-empty jug of water. Yeah, that little bastard. He'll get his when we get back."

With a dark cloud over his head, he rode on, kicking his horse into a trot, then a gallop. He wanted to get there, intimidate somebody new, have something else to do besides ride that damn horse.

They'd been underway for three days and Sawyer Brown was angry that they weren't there yet. He was ready to engage with this community, let them feel the heat of his ire.

Talking about heat, the scouts rode a quarter mile in front of the others. They waved and pointed. Sawyer continued riding ahead, squinting where they were pointing. A lean tendril of smoke drifted skyward from a small cabin. In the distance, he could see what looked like a streetlight. Sawyer checked the sun's position. It was over the mountains to the west, but would soon disappear behind them. He wanted to sleep in a bed that night. Smoke meant humans.

They'd found the settlement.

"To that cabin. We go in fast. You two, inside as soon as we get there and pull out whoever you find. I want to talk with them." He waved the others ahead and followed slowly. He had lackeys to do his bidding. Just in case the locals had weapons, his people would bear the brunt of any armed defense.

As it was, the people weren't armed. When his two men stormed inside, they found a man and woman sitting at a dining room table, just finishing their dinner. The table was thrown aside as the man attempted to fight the intruders, but they were too much for him and in moments, they dragged him and the woman outside and threw them into the straggly grass of the front yard.

"Terry Henry is going to have your ass!" the man howled hysterically, the whites of his eyes showing his fear.

Sawyer rode close, kicking his horse until it bumped the man. Sawyer started to lean down to say something smart, but could not come up with anything, so he settled for kicking the man in the face. He went down like a sack of potatoes while the woman looked on, too terrified to scream.

The big man climbed down from his horse and approached the woman. He sniffed her and it made her skin crawl. He grabbed her arms and pulled her off her feet. She produced a knife and stabbed at his chest, but she didn't have enough movement with her arms to do any damage. Sawyer looked down at the weapon.

"A fighter, huh. I like it when they fight," he said. The man had regained his feet, unseen as Sawyer's posse watched their boss zero in on his target. The man hit Sawyer Brown with a full body block, but Sawyer was a big man. He teetered, but didn't go down. He grabbed the man and twisted him around in a circle. Sawyer wrapped a massive arm around the smaller man's neck. He lifted and twisted, letting the man's weight and gravity work in conjunction with his own physical power. The man's neck snapped with a loud crack.

The woman screamed and turned her knife around and plunged it into her own throat. Sawyer Brown lunged, but it was too late. All he managed to do was get covered in blood as the woman's carotid spurted her life in great red arcs. In fifteen seconds, she was down, and in less than a minute, she was dead.

"What the hell were you doing, dickless?" Sawyer yelled at the man who was supposed to be holding her. He grabbed him by his collar and dragged him forward, thrusting his face toward the woman's dead body. "Look at that! Wasted because you couldn't do your job. I ought to kill you! You ruined my evening," Sawyer bellowed.

"I'm sorry, boss, it was all my fault. I'll do better next time, honest!" the man cried and pleaded.

Sawyer threw him to the side. Clyde started licking the woman's blood. Sawyer watched for second, then nudged the dog away. "Now, now, Clyde. I don't want you to get a taste for humans. You sleep too close to me, buddy. Get away from there!" Sawyer yelled at the dog until he convinced the mutt to go inside with him.

There was still food warming on the side of a wood-burning stove. He sniffed it and took the whole pan to the table. He wiped off one of the used forks on his pants leg and dug in. Some kind of wild game in a stew with crisp vegetables. He hadn't had a meal like that in a long time. Damn! The woman was dead. If she could cook like that then having her around would have been multifaceted. He'd threatened his boys to make sure nothing like that happened again.

It never occurred to Sawyer Brown that maybe the man was the cook. Sawyer had been raised a certain way, and it benefitted him to maintain that stereotype in his mind.

It made it easy to kill the men and comfortable to treat the women as property.

As he ate, he wondered who this Terry Henry was. He looked forward to meeting the man that the corpse put so much faith in. He didn't save that man, and he wouldn't save anyone else.

"Fuck 'em," Sawyer said as he sat back and belched. The padded chair felt good. He looked at the loft. He hated ladders, but there was a real bed up there. He'd be sleeping well tonight. "Sorry, Clyde. I'm not going to carry your ass up there. You're sleeping down here tonight. At least they have a couch," he said, trying to console his only friend.

Sawyer opened the back door, relieved himself without stepping outside, then closed the door behind him as he returned inside. He sniffed the air. The smell of stew and wildflowers filled the cabin. It was humble and clean, a place that people cared about. The dead out front had been those people.

He started digging through drawers and in the closet,

determining quickly that they had nothing he wanted beside their bed.

Sawyer cracked the front door and saw his men, milling about, disorganized. "Hey, Jagoff! Set up security around this house, half on, half off, through the night. And for fuck's sake, get rid of those bodies!" he bellowed. With eight men, he wanted four on watch at any time. He'd let the men sort it out. If he woke in the middle of the night, he'd go for a walk, find someone sleeping, and beat the hell out of them. Then he'd get a drink.

It was his way.

❖ ❖ ❖

Margie Rose cooked a big breakfast for her two houseguests, who sat at the table, conspicuously not looking at each other. The old lady sat down heavily and rapped her wooden spoon on the table. Terry had his rifle, pistol, and bullwhip. Who was he to deny Margie Rose her weapon of choice?

"What is with you two?" she demanded. Terry looked at his eggs and venison sausage. Char gave up trying to make eye contact with him. The purple of her eyes was vivid in the morning sun streaming through the kitchen window. Margie Rose sighed as she wondered how any woman could be so striking.

"We have to protect you, Margie Rose. We have to protect all the people here. What Terry showed me yesterday is that I'm not as good at fighting as I thought I was. Terry is trying to train his men, and I'm going to join them. I spent a great deal of time while I was in the mountains fighting, and I got good, but not good enough, not good enough to save you. With electricity, with food, with happy people... Yeah. Bad men will come and we have to be ready. I have to be ready." Char played with the food on her plate, started to push it away, then changed her mind, and shoveled the rest into her mouth.

Terry finished and sat back. Margie Rose continued to eye them both intently. "So that's it, huh? Training to fight some non-existent enemy? Why can't you two just give in, get married, and start growing this community the natural way," she implored them. Terry swallowed heavily. Char didn't look up, but kicked him under the table. He grunted with the impact.

She's a Werewolf, Terry said in his mind as he looked to reply to Margie Rose. "I think we'll keep things professional for now. We're heading out into the wasteland, see what's out there, see what the threat is. If the world is a safe place, then we can look at other options. In the interim, your safety comes first, Margie Rose." Terry smiled and rubbed the old lady's arm. She frowned, but ended up nodding.

"For now. Professional, you say. Options, you say, as if love was some kind of contract. Bah!" She used the spoon to point at the both of them. "Coal for both of you for Christmas." She pushed away from the table in a huff and pounded her way back into the kitchen.

Char snickered.

"We've got a bit of a run to get there. I expect you're faster than me, so take it easy. I can't look like I'm ready to die when I introduce you to the first members of the Force de Guerre," he said proudly.

"The what?" she asked sarcastically. "And why would you think I can outrun you? You're the big man. I'm just a dainty woman and all," she toyed. He didn't bite on the bait she dangled.

"I've seen you move, and I'm a good judge of people. That's all."

"You're watching me, you sly dog!" she taunted him

further. He got up, took his dishes into the kitchen, and kissed Margie Rose on her forehead. Then he went to the stove, removed the kettle of perpetually hot water, and readied the dishwater. Margie Rose chased him and Char away, all the time lamenting the fact that she was never going to see grandchildren. Terry didn't mention that neither he nor Char were her kids, but he didn't want to burst her bubble.

Margie Rose may have been dismayed that her adopted daughter was a Werewolf, and possibly a man-killer. Terry had no way of knowing that she wasn't the one who had half-eaten the hunter he found in the mountains. She was in the pack that did it, but how many were there? And where were they?

He shook his head and pursed his lips. Too many questions and the person with the answers couldn't know that he knew her secret. The not knowing would chap his ass, but winning her over to his side would be a step in the right direction. Selfishly, he needed her speed and strength. He only had four people and none of them would survive in combat with a determined enemy.

He resigned himself to the fact that one of his recruits was a Werewolf. At least with her, he wouldn't need to train anyone in combat medicine. He'd read the full book. It was fascinating and although he wanted to try some of the surgical techniques within, he figured it was best not to slice people open. He practiced whenever he gutted a deer.

He figured it was close enough for government work.

When he and Char left the house, he set the initial pace, but she inched ahead, increasing her speed a little at a time until they were almost sprinting when they arrived at the barracks. His chest heaved and he sucked in great quantities of air while she barely breathed hard. The four men quickly exited the building and stopped when they saw Terry's company.

Then the preening began as they postured to get a better look at the tall, beautiful woman standing before them.

"Get in formation!" Terry yelled. They lined up and stood tall, but couldn't keep from darting glances her way. "You, too!" he growled at Char. She ran to the end, going in front of each man instead of behind. Terry wanted to grab her by the throat. "Eyes front, gentlemen," he told them in an even tone.

"Which one of you is the best in hand-to-hand combat?" Terry asked, deciding he needed to make his point early. The others looked at the big man, Jim. He raised his hand sheepishly. "Get out here."

Jim walked forward, cracking his knuckles and stretching. He assumed a fighting pose and warily watched Terry, who had kicked Jim's ass upside and backwards on every occasion.

"Oh no. Not me. Her." He pointed with his thumb. "Get out here and square off." Jim relaxed, and Terry was instantly in the big man's face.

"You better get your wits about you if you don't want to die. Do you understand me? She's faster than you, and she's stronger than you. She's better than you. I give you five seconds and you'll be on the ground wondering what happened," Terry spit at Jim and walked away in feigned disgust.

Char strolled out of formation and assumed a loose fighting position. "Let me introduce you to Private Charumati, called Char. You will treat her as you treat anyone in the FDG, with respect and professionalism. Anything else will result in what you are about to witness."

Jim crouched lower, unsure of the reason for the ominous buildup. He took a cautious step forward, then another.

She backed up a step. Jim instantly grew overconfident and waded into battle.

When he reached out to grab her, she charged forward, caught his arm in one hand, and seized him by the throat with the other. She picked him off the ground and continued moving forward, carrying him backward until she body slammed him in the grass. He grunted. For good measure, she punched him in the mouth, just a quick jab, but enough to split his lip and send blood splattering over his face.

She bowed and casually walked back to the end of the line. No one watched her pass this time. They were still looking at Jim, lying on the ground and moaning.

"Gentlemen, that's what pure power looks like. It is more important than strength. Did you see how she used leverage to overwhelm her larger opponent? Did you see her speed? Jim was distracted by the way she looks. Don't be. When you face an opponent, all you need to see are strengths and weaknesses. Devlin, get out here, you're next. Char?"

The Werewolf stepped back onto the sparse grass and dandelions that made up the front yard of the barracks. They'd done enough calisthenics on the ad hoc lawn to keep it crushed down, but it still provided more cushion than some of the desertscape of the area. It was an odd mix of ground coverings in New Boulder.

Devlin moved cautiously, hands up defensively, afraid as he could only stare at Char's purple eyes. Terry jumped in between the two and stopped the bout. Char was working some Werewolf trick on Devlin and Terry wouldn't have it. He pointed at her and waved his finger back and forth. "Now be ready!" he barked at Devlin. The young man shook the cobwebs out of his brain, gritted his teeth, and clenched his fists.

Terry stepped away and turned them loose. Without

hesitation, Char bolted forward, faking low, stopping instantly, and jumping straight in the air. She spun and delivered a roundhouse kick to the side of Devlin's head.

When he woke up, he couldn't remember anything besides seeing her start to run at him. The rest was a gray haze.

Ivan looked shocked and terrified while Mark held up his hands in surrender.

"I think we'll call those lessons learned. Grab your gear. We're going to the rifle range. Get up, you idiots," Terry yelled at the two men weaving as they sat in the grass.

❖ ❖ ❖

"Billy, I declare, you are a new man!" Felicity drawled seductively as she snipped his hair with a freshly sharpened pair of scissors, cleaning up his raggedy mane. He never thought about his hair or how it made him look, but Felicity insisted, which seemed to be more and more of his life lately. But he begrudgingly admitted that his life was getting better with each day. He was eating better, feeling better, and as much as he liked a good beat down, he was good with not delivering one. He'd lost his best crew because of Terry Henry Walton. Now they were shaping up to be a military force.

"Hey, let's go visit the FDG," Billy suggested. Felicity put the scissors down and carefully removed the apron around Billy's shoulders. She then straddled his lap and looked at him closely.

"I'm glad you're taking this seriously, Billy dear. This is going to be the first of the great towns in a new country and you, Billy dear, are going to run them all. It's what you were born to do." She held his gaze and finally stepped back, pulling him to his feet.

"Maybe I was," he conceded. "We shall see."

They drank plenty of water before leaving the house. It was a hot summer, but nothing worse than usual. They felt like the temperatures had cooled, but no one kept track of that stuff anymore. Maybe they were getting used to it. The farmers seemed to have adjusted the quickest by using irrigation, water misters, and a ventilation system to cool the greenhouses in the summers. Without those, everything would be scorched, wilt, and die.

Electricity and powered fans would further improve the cooling capacity of the greenhouses and delivery of water.

Dammit! Billy thought. *Look what I've become, a city planner, a bureaucrat.*

Dammit to hell!

"Terry Henry had it right. He wanted to be the security chief because he wouldn't be trapped in an office doing office stuff, thinking office things," Billy told Felicity. She nodded knowingly. "He said he needed me. I thought he was smart, but the man is a damned genius. No one in their right mind would want this job."

He laughed as he headed out, walking fast, because that's just what they did. Billy had not had good luck with horses, although Felicity was trying to get him to reconsider. She did not like walking.

As they walked, she skipped on occasion to keep up. It was only a mile, but Billy seemed determined to make it to the barracks in fifteen minutes. Five minutes in, they saw the small formation running on a hillside not far away. They turned toward the hills and ran into the distance.

"Was there five people besides Walton?" Billy asked. Felicity shrugged. She'd seen, and she recognized that last person in line. It did not bring her comfort and joy.

Char had joined the boys.

❖ ❖ ❖

Sawyer Brown woke up in a foul mood. The bed was too soft and his back hurt. His seat was still sore from the saddle and he was hungry.

"Smeghead!" he howled out the door as he let Clyde out to run around the dirt and scrub. Sawyer had planned on getting up in the middle of the night so he could catch his boys sleeping, but he didn't make it. It was already morning and not even early morning, judging by the sun's position in the eastern sky.

The man affectionately known as "Smeghead" ran to the door.

"Morning! What's up, boss?" the man asked, trying to be pleasant, but prepared for an ass-kicking if that was what Sawyer Brown determined the man needed.

"Get me some chow and then saddle the horses. We're moving out. How come nobody woke me?" he bellowed, a rhetorical question as he'd almost killed a man once who had woken him, on Sawyer's own orders. He was not a morning person.

The men had killed a couple rabbits during the night and they were cooking over a small fire. Smeghead looked back forlornly. One to the boss and one for the other eight men. Same as usual. He couldn't wait to get into town and find real food, maybe even someone to cook it.

He ran off to grab the mostly cooked rabbit, assuming that speed took precedence over quality.

He brought the skewer with the rabbit back, holding it high over his head because Clyde wanted some of that action and was jumping after it. Smeghead couldn't get rid of the rabbit quickly enough. If he lost that one to the dog, then the men would go hungry. It would not have been the first time.

Sawyer took the rabbit and grunted, holding Clyde outside with a foot as he closed the door, so he could eat it in peace.

"Saddle the horses!" the man yelled to the others and watched Clyde bolt past him on his way to the fire. "And stop that dog!"

❖ ❖ ❖

The walk became longer than Billy expected, but the air was clear and it was shaping up to be a nice day. Felicity stopped complaining and seemed to be enjoying the walk as well.

"What was this place, Billy dear?" she asked, genuinely interested after having lived there for a year.

"This was the suburbs of Boulder in what used to be the state of Colorado. You know, we could smoke weed back then, legally. Now that there are no laws, no one cares. Man, what I wouldn't give for a joint right now. The stuff has to grow wild somewhere around here, doesn't it?"

"A joint? What are you, twelve? Billy dear, we're not going to look for any magical weeds that you can smoke. I will not have the house smelling like burnt weeds!" Felicity stated, putting her foot down.

Billy laughed.

"Weed, not weeds. It leaves an earthy smell that I think you'd like. I'll keep my eye out, see if any of it is still around," Billy said hopefully. Felicity set her mouth and shook her head vigorously. "Or not," he added after her display.

He still kept his eyes peeled.

The small formation had disappeared around a bend that led to a cut in the hillside. Billy wasn't sure what they would be doing there, but figured he'd find out soon enough.

As they reached the junction, he could hear Terry yelling and the men yelling back. One female voice was almost drowned out in the chorus. Billy had been walking fast, but this encouraged him to walk even faster. Felicity jogged to keep pace. Before they could see the security team, they heard the sound of rifle fire. Too many cracks. Were they using up all their ammunition?

Billy broke into a sprint, but slid to a stop as soon as he saw. Mark and Devlin aimed their rifles at a spot on the hill. Terry cracked his whip over their heads as they practiced firing without flinching. Billy and Felicity watched as the others held aiming poses, but without weapons.

Terry stopped when he saw the intruders.

"Up!" he yelled. They responded with "yes, sir" and assumed a position of attention, even Char.

Billy walked with a swagger until Felicity grabbed his arm, digging her nails deeply into his flesh. The exchange was not lost on Terry. *She's a Werewolf, dickhead*, Terry thought, laughing inside as Billy couldn't help himself.

"Firearms training. I see. Is that for when you have more ammunition?" Billy asked.

"Indeed," Terry replied cautiously. The mayor's conversation was going somewhere and Terry couldn't fathom that it led anywhere good.

"Maybe your training time would be more beneficial if you practiced with what you do have and not with what you might have," Billy demeaned, impressing his position of self-proclaimed superiority.

Terry only looked at him, not countering Billy in front of the others, but not supporting him either. Billy squinted, ready for a retort, but Char spoke up first.

"What's that?" she asked, pointing. Black oily smoke boiled in the distance, but not too far away. Terry ran toward a small hill that blocked the source of the fire and raced upward. Billy and Char were close on his heels.

Once there, he tried to find the best vantage point to look between the trees. He couldn't tell for sure, as the fire was miles away. "Char, look through here. What do you see?" Her Werewolf eyes were better than his. Billy's natural human eyes paled in comparison to the other two.

"A small cabin is burning close to what used to be the highway. I see people on horses, riding this way," she said.

"How can you see all that?" Billy asked. Terry ignored him as he bolted. Char took off running as well, leaving Billy on the hillside, squinting into the distance.

"Listen up!" Terry ordered. "We have men on horseback. They just burned a cabin on the edge of town. The only thing between them and our people is us. We have buildings to protect and people to defend. I'll think about our deployment as we head in. But we have to go, now, if we are to beat them into position. In formation!" Terry yelled. As soon as they were standing tall, he took off running. They followed without question.

Ivan started to breathe heavily before they'd run the first one hundred yards, so Terry slowed, then pulled him out of their small formation. "Go with Billy and Felicity, protect them. Make sure they get back home. Billy needs to load up and be ready. Now, go!" Terry slapped him on the back and sent the man away. He wasn't ready for a fight. At least the others could probably hold their own, although Terry didn't consider them to be ready either.

They took off running again, and Devlin set the pace. Terry drifted back until he was even with Char, where he whispered so only she could hear.

"I'll place them in a position to protect us if we get over-run, but you and I will meet them head on. You good with that?"

"Yeah. They won't know what hit them," she whispered back.

"That's what I'm thinking," Terry replied.

He told Devlin to maintain the pace as Terry ran ahead, then dove left, onto a small rise where he could get a better look at their situation. Nine people on horses, maybe a mile away, were heading up the main road, bunched up as if they didn't have a care in the world. Terry sprinted off the hill and directed Devlin to set up on the right flank behind a small wall of rocks. Terry gave him ten rounds of ammunition in one magazine.

He put Jim with his pistol on the main road, behind an old rusted hulk that had been a pickup truck.

Terry told Mark to head another quarter mile perpendicular to the newcomers' avenue of approach and protect the left flank. He gave him a magazine with ten rounds. "If you shoot, make every shot count. Sight alignment. Sight picture. Breathe out and squeeze. Go." Mark ran off.

Char stayed with Terry. "Do you want a knife or something?" he asked.

"Nope. I'm good," she replied. He thought he saw fire in her eyes, but it was only for a moment. If she needed to change into a Werewolf during the fight, he wouldn't begrudge her that. Whatever it took. This was the deadly serious part of being the security chief. Winning was all that mattered. The only fair fight is the one you lose.

He nodded and started walking down the road toward the incoming mob.

CHAPTER ELEVEN

oss," Harold called. Once Sawyer turned toward him, the man pointed ahead. A man and a woman were walking toward them on the road.

Sawyer Brown watched for a moment. "He's armed. Spread out, you idiots," he called. The ditches along the side of the road were filled with debris. Broken down fences blocked most of the way out of the ditch. Two men went left, picking their way through until they were beyond and in a relatively open area. They rode ahead quickly until they were abreast the two people Two men went to the right, but they couldn't get through. They settled for riding as close to the ditch as possible.

Sawyer gave up and spurred his horse forward until he was right behind Harold and Smeghead, ensuring they shielded him in case any shooting started. The man and woman finally stopped walking. The man's rifle was slung differently than what Sawyer was used to seeing. It hung under his arm, casually, yet ready to fire. He wore other gear that made him look like a soldier from days past. Sawyer called his men to a halt.

The woman was striking and once Sawyer saw her, everything else he'd been thinking about disappeared. He was close enough to see her purple eyes and brown hair, the silver streak on one side. She was tall and shapely. She carried nothing, and like the man, she stood easy, confident, unconcerned about the armed and dangerous men before her.

"Ho there, friend," Sawyer called. The two didn't move. The woman looked to her right where two horses with Sawyer's riders stood still, watching from the side. "I said, ho, friend." Sawyer repeated, as he slowly removed one pistol from its holster.

❖ ❖ ❖

"What business do you have here?" Terry Henry asked, all the while assessing the enemy. He'd seen the big man loosen his pistol and then hold it in his lap. He also noted how the big man positioned himself behind the two in the lead. A bully. A coward. *You die first, fucker*, Terry thought.

"We are looking to trade, that's all, friend. Who am I talking with?" the man offered, but he wasn't convincing as a trader. "Shut up, Clyde!" the big man added as the dog on the road barked and growled, keeping his attention fixed solely on Charumati.

"That's different. I thought you were coming to try and take what we have, but if you're willing to trade, then I'm sure we can work something out. Put all your weapons and ammunition on the ground and we'll see you get as much food as you can carry."

The big man snorted as he gently stroked his pistol, a 9mm Glock, if Terry wasn't mistaken.

"By the way, friend," Terry said, making the word "friend" a pejorative, "a nice, young couple lived in that cabin that just burned down. You wouldn't happen to know anything about that, would you?" Terry taunted. He turned his head just enough to hide that he was whispering out the corner of his mouth. "Take the two in the field, when I fire."

Char nodded almost imperceptibly. She could smell the men's thoughts of lust. It sickened her. She started shaking with anticipation of an impending kill. *C'mon, TH, shoot him already. Let's get this party started!* she encouraged within the confines of her own mind.

"Nah. It was burning when we rode past. Nothing we could do, so we kept on," the big man parried.

"I'm Terry Henry Walton, security chief for New Boulder, and who may I have the pleasure of addressing?" Terry continued to size up the tactical situation. Seven were bunched on the road, two in front, two partially blocked near the ditch, the big man hiding, and two more further back. Then there were the two in the field. Nine total men, most armed with Kalashnikovs. The big man carried two small pistols. He was clearly their leader. Terry wondered how dedicated the others would be to the fight when their boss was lying dead on the ground.

"I'm Sawyer Brown and these are my boys. We come from a small place south of Denver," Sawyer replied, giving the same that he received. "Clyde!" he yelled again. The mutt stood with its hackles up, growling and baring its fangs.

"Well, Sawyer Brown, how about we go back to that cabin and see how things are, talk to that couple, make sure they're okay." One of the men in front of him snickered, then covered his mouth as he darted glances back to his boss and forward to Terry.

"I don' think there's any need to do that. I think that fine lady should come closer and say hi to me," Sawyer said, ogling Char appreciatively. His boys also looked at the woman. Terry glanced from one to the next. No eyes were on him. He smoothly pulled his .45 and held it behind his leg.

"What do you think, Char? I can go right if you want to go talk with the big man?" Terry said, hoping she got his meaning. She turned and winked at Terry, before sauntering forward. She walked between the two men acting as a shield for their boss. As she passed, she trailed a single finger down each of their legs, not looking up to see the effect it had on them.

Clyde backed up slowly and started to bark again.

Terry watched it all, stuffing the pistol into his pocket as he readied his rifle. The two closest men turned their backs on him as they watched Char approach Sawyer Brown. The big man was licking his lips, eyes wide in anticipation.

❖ ❖ ❖

Billy set the pace as they jogged back to his house. Ivan seemed to be keeping up with no problem, a huge change from only recently. Felicity didn't like walking and downright despised running. She struggled through only because of the threat to their lives. Billy hurried the small group. He wanted to be armed and swore that he'd never leave the house again without carrying a weapon. It was embarrassing to be running and not have a rifle with him.

Once they were close, Billy yelled over his shoulder. "I'm running to get my rifle, and I'll cover you as you make it the last bit." Felicity took that as her cue to walk. Billy left them behind as he raced for the house, straight through the front door, and to the armory. He opened it and left it unlocked as he jammed a magazine into the slot of his AK-74 and pulled the bolt back, letting it ram a cartridge into the chamber. He raced upstairs, opened the window, and looked out. He couldn't see what he wanted to see. A tree and a lone house blocked his sight of the road approaching from the south.

The black smoke from the cabin fire continued to drift skyward, lighter now, but still there. The last of the wooden timbers had held out as long as they could, Billy surmised, and now they were giving in, turning to ash and coals.

He shook his head in disbelief as Felicity and Ivan walked toward the house, chatting as if on a Sunday stroll. "Would you two idiots get in here!" Billy yelled. Felicity stopped where she was and slowly dialed up her middle finger that she thrust in the air at him. Then they started walking again.

"Ivan! Go grab the shotgun from the armory and watch out back," Billy ordered. Ivan jogged forward and entered the house, not waiting to hold the door for Felicity. She walked in, closing the door behind her and locking it once inside.

Time for you to earn your keep, Terry Henry Walton, she thought. *Those men had best not make it here.*

❖ ❖ ❖

Terry looked quickly about, using just his eyes so the enemy wouldn't see movement until it was too late. He confirmed that the enemy were all looking at Char. It was time.

Terry dropped to a knee and fired at one of the men in the field on their right flank. The man went down. The second horse bucked. Terry waited until all four hooves hit the dirt, then he squeezed the trigger. He didn't wait to see the second man fall. Terry was a sitting duck if he stayed in the middle of the road. He assumed the rest of Sawyer's gang would attack, so he dove forward, off the road, and rolled into the ditch.

At the sound of the shot, Sawyer snapped his head up to see who fired. Char took two steps and leaped. The big man started to raise his pistol but he was too late. Char flew at him, rotating her trunk to add power to her right-handed jab. She hit him in the face with everything she had, but he was the biggest man she'd ever tackled. He rocked backward, then slowly tumbled from his horse. Char bounced off him and spun away, landing lightly on the ground.

The men up front were fumbling with their weapons, and she couldn't see where TH had gone, so that was the direction she decided to go. She ran toward the two between her and Terry, grabbing an arm of each man and yanking them from their saddles. When they hit the ground, she kicked one in the face and seized the other by his head, savagely twisting it around. She broke his neck and dumped him where he died. She throat-punched the first man so hard, she felt his spine with her knuckles. The man flopped in his death throes, unable to take a breath through his crushed windpipe.

Char dodged behind the horses as a shot rang out from behind her. Then a second. Terry returned fire from the ditch, but only once. He was too limited on ammunition to fire without having a clean shot.

Char guided the scared horses toward the two men at the side of the ditch. She slapped the horses hard, driving them before her. They ran into the other two, and she bolted around them, heading for one of the two men. He pointed his rifle at her, but she was too close and struck the end of the barrel with her hand as he fired. The bullet whizzed past her ear as the blast deafened her. She ripped the rifle from the man's hand as the butt of another rifle crashed into the back of her head.

Sparks and stars was all she saw as she stumbled forward, bumped against the horse, and started to fall. A rough hand grabbed her and started to drag her upward. She screamed and it turned into a howl as she involuntarily changed into her Werewolf form. She raked the man's arm with her claws and then bit his face. The Werewolf kicked off the horse and flipped backwards, landing with all four paws in the middle of the second man's chest.

❖ ❖ ❖

"What the hell is going on? I can't see anything, I'm going up to the attic," Billy said, frantic at the sound of gunfire. He ran for the access, pulling down the folding ladder, and quickly climbing into the hot, dry attic. He scrambled upward and into the dark, where he had to wait until he could see enough to not fall through the ceiling. There were boards placed across the ceiling runners that he carefully negotiated to get to the window. Once there, he flung it open and looked out. Finally, he could see into the distance, but it was far enough away that he couldn't make out details.

He could hear the firing, but couldn't tell who was doing it. The volume of fire suggested that it wasn't Terry's men. They didn't have the ammunition for it.

He watched what looked like a skirmish on the main road. Two horses were prancing in a field to the right of the road. To the left was another open field, but there were no horses out there. He thought he saw men running in the fields, but couldn't be sure who they were.

There was something going on with four horses wedged tightly into one area. He waited for them to separate so he could try to figure out what happened.

❖ ❖ ❖

As the Werewolf crashed into him, the man tried to cover his head with his arm, but Char clamped her jaws on it and bit through his forearm. With a shake of her head, she ripped that part of his arm free. He screamed in panic as she dragged him from the horse and hauled him bodily into the ditch, where she tore his body apart in her rage. Once the bloodlust settled, she changed back into human form and looked for her clothes, which were torn and covered in blood and dirt.

Terry watched Char as she changed, but only briefly as he had the last two men to deal with. Those two were firing as if ammunition was easy to come by. He kept his head down as bullets pinged and splattered all around him. When he was able to get off a shot, it wasn't well aimed. He hated to waste it, but he had to do something. With Char engaged, he was on his own. Then he saw the rifles in the road from the first two men Char had killed. He decided to leave cover when he heard other shots coming from the field.

Mark was running on one side and Devlin, the other. They were shooting while running, an ill-advised tactic, but it distracted the last of Sawyer's men and gave Terry the opening he needed. He jumped from the ditch, ran two steps, and dove for the closest rifle. He flipped it off safe, aimed, and fired.

Click.

He looked at it. Although a magazine was seated, the rifle hadn't been loaded. He frantically searched for ammunition while lying prone in the road. While Terry was digging through the pockets of the dead, Sawyer Brown came to his senses enough to act. He used the saddle's stirrup to help pull himself to his feet. He crawled onto his horse's back and yanked the beast's head around as he spurred it back south. With Sawyer's horse out of the way, Terry found himself exposed in the middle of the road. The two men took aim, but their horses were dancing as they watched their boss race past.

Terry rolled back toward the ditch as the last two men turned and followed their fleeing leader. When Terry crawled from the ditch and aimed his M4 at the retreating forms, something bumped his leg. He jumped back, only to find Clyde at his feet, looking at him, panting and wagging his tail.

Mark and Devlin fired a couple more times, but Terry yelled at them through cupped hands to stop wasting ammunition.

"Catch those horses!" He pointed at Devlin as the young man ran through the field. He slowed, slung his rifle over his shoulder, and walked slowly toward the animals, holding his hands up and trying not to spook the horses any more than they already were.

Terry picked up the rifles and scoured the bodies for ammunition, pleased with what he was able to amass. The first rifle he recovered, the one he tried to fire, was bad. It had a broken firing pin. But he could use it for parts for the other rifles, all AK-47s, which fired the 7.62 x 39mm round. Between the four men on the ground, there were hundreds of rounds of ammunition and three working rifles.

Mark worked his way through the ditch and looked oddly at Char, finally approaching her and asking if she was okay. Her clothes were torn, disheveled, and covered in blood. She looked as if she'd been attacked and violated, but she assured him that wasn't the case. Terry handed the weapons and ammunition to Mark.

Terry approached Char. "Are you all right?" he asked, concerned after Mark had just had the same question. He'd heard the shot, but didn't know if she'd been hit.

"I'm fine, just got a little over-exuberant, shall we say? Did you see…?" she asked.

"See what?" He pointed down the road. "I was occupied with the Ballslappy McAsshats that got away." Terry looked down the road at the dust from the retreating horses and clenched his jaw.

She didn't need to know that he knew.

Each of the men who escaped was someone they'd have to fight again. "We have rifles, ammunition, and horses. I think we need to follow those asswipes, all the way to their home, and then clean out the nest of snakes," Terry hissed.

"Where's Jim?" Terry asked, looking at Mark. He pointed down the road to the position Jim had been assigned and started waving. Soon they could see the larger man jogging toward them.

Devlin rode one horse and led the other as he negotiated his way from the field, through the fence and ditch, and onto the road.

Terry reassessed the tactical situation. Six enemy down, no friendlies injured. Three escaped, including the leader and that was a major shortcoming. Five rifles and one shotgun recovered. Four rifles functional. Once they checked the saddlebags, they found more ammunition, an entire brick—about a thousand rounds for the AK-47s. They only found four shells for the 12-gauge. And then there were the six horses.

The men carried nothing remarkable besides their weapons. The saddles were rough but functional, and the horses looked lean, leaner than they should have been.

Terry wanted to leave that instant to follow Sawyer Brown and finish him, but the horses were in poor shape and he needed to train his men on how to use their new rifles. He also wanted to conduct an after action, teach them how to train themselves to be better by reviewing every single action taken during the engagement.

No time like the present.

They removed the saddles and let the horses graze along the ditch where the grasses were growing fairly well. Terry brought his people together in a circle. Clyde barked and snapped at Char. When she'd had enough, her hand lashed out and grabbed the dog by the scruff of its neck. She picked it up and held it before her face. She bared her teeth and yelled in its face.

The dog went limp, whimpering. She put it back down, gently. "Now shut up, you dumb dog," she cautioned. Clyde slinked away until he was behind Terry Henry.

"I guess we know who the alpha is," Mark said.

Char's head rocketed up and she glared at him. "What did you say?" she demanded, although she'd heard clearly.

"Nothing. Nothing at all," he countered.

The alpha. She liked the sound of that. Maybe she'd take care of business when her pack returned. They needed a new alpha, and with what TH was going to teach her, she'd be ready to deal with Marcus when the time came.

"Listen up, we're going to walk through this engagement, talk about every aspect of it, what we liked, what we didn't like, and what we need to do better. This review will establish our training plan until we can make sure those horses are healthy. And then we go after one Sawyer Brown and make sure he never bothers us again..."

CHAPTER TWELVE

What the fuck was that?" Sawyer demanded. One eye was swollen shut and his face hurt like never before. He figured the bone around his eye was broken. He could barely touch it.

They were standing around, only a few miles from where they had the displeasure of meeting Terry Henry Walton.

"How many of them were there?" he asked, the whole episode a blur in his mind.

"I only saw the two, then a bunch more came running, caught us in a crossfire. We were outnumbered and outgunned, boss. Nothing we could do," brown-noser said, hoping to placate the big man.

"That fucking bitch! She'll be sorry she didn't kill me. I will have her. We're going home to get the rest of my boys and then we'll be back. She'll be mine and that Terry Henry cockwad will be pushing up daisies," Sawyer snarled. His horse had fallen over and died, pushed too hard. He'd taken one of the others and made his last two men double-up.

"What happened to Clyde? Where's my dog?" He grabbed the others, one in each hand. They only shook their heads. "If they killed my dog, then I'll see that they die real slow. There's no room in this world for dog-killers," Sawyer threatened. "He knew something was wrong with that bitch. He was onto her at the start. Shoulda listened to my dog. He was smarter than any of you idiots." Sawyer climbed on the tired horse and started riding, expecting the other men to catch up.

He was pushing the horses and pushing his men because that was the first fight he'd ever lost, and he was afraid.

He lost a fight to a woman and badly. He lost six of his men, too, and their horses and weapons. He grumbled to himself as he looked for a place to water the horses and let them feed.

He knew he couldn't keep pushing, but if the security chief and his posse came after them, they wouldn't be able to fight them off. With eight of his men he couldn't fight them off. It would be impossible with only two.

He pushed on, but not as fast as he wanted to. Even as angry as he was, he was smart enough not to kill another horse.

Sawyer looked around as they rode. "Off the road, toward the hills. Let's hole up in that stand of trees over there. Plenty of green. Looks like there's a stream. Water and food for the horses. They rest and then we head home," Sawyer spilled in a stream of consciousness. He didn't know why his brain wasn't working right, but something was wrong. He just couldn't think straight.

All he wanted to do was sleep.

❖ ❖ ❖

Terry sent Mark and Jim to the burning cabin, to verify what he already knew. They rode their newly acquired horses, but slowly, keeping things calm until they were sure that they, both human and animal, were ready. With Devlin and Char, Terry took the weaponry, ammunition and the last four horses into town. He needed to bring Billy Spires up to speed.

They rode in silence. Char looked a hot mess, but she wasn't injured. Clyde ran along between Terry and Char. The straggly mutt was a short hair, white with brown spots and big, hound ears. He dug through his memory and thought that the dog looked like an oversized coonhound. He bellowed like one, as they had found out when the mutt first saw Char.

The dog assumed its rightful place in its new pack's pecking order. It was appropriately submissive to the Werewolf. He wondered how Char felt about having a dog. Judging by the look on her face, she was not pleased at all.

For Terry, that meant Clyde was his new best friend.

"We need to get you cleaned up before we see Billy. They don't need to see you like this," Terry said, wondering where they'd get clothes.

"I'm fine, just give me that blanket." Char pointed to one tied to the saddle on the horse he rode. Char's horse bucked and whinnied while she was near it, but it settled down as they continued to ride. None of the animals liked Werewolves.

Go figure.

With the blanket wrapped around her, Terry declared it good enough and they rode to the mayor's house, where they found Billy Spires looking out an upstairs window, his rifle conspicuously aimed their way. When he was certain who it was, Billy disappeared inside, soon reappearing through the front door with both Ivan and Felicity close on his heels.

"Raiders," Terry started. "Nine total. Three got away and we'll be going after them soon, once these horses have rested and recovered." Terry climbed down and pointed to the weapons. "We secured four functioning AK-47s and about a thousand rounds of ammo. I'd like to keep these for my people and the M4 for me."

Billy nodded, but his eyes were locked on Char with a look of horror.

Terry stepped in front of Billy, to block his sight. "None of that blood is hers. She killed four of them herself. Her clothes suffered, but none of them touched her. She distracted them, and that gave us the edge," Terry told him, then turned to Felicity. "Could you find something for her to wear, something that's not torn and covered in blood? Please, Felicity?" Terry looked her in the eyes, pleading.

She relented, nodding reluctantly, then waved at Char to follow her into the house. The men watched the two go, unable to help themselves.

When the door closed, Terry, Billy, and the others turned their attention to the engagement. Terry walked him through the entire two minutes in nauseating detail. Billy wanted to know more, specifically where the men came from and how Terry was going to keep them from returning.

"We'll find them. I promise that we'll hunt them down and convince the big man that not returning is in his best interest," Terry stated firmly.

"How are you going to do that? From what you described, I expect the only thing he'll think about is to come back here. For Christ's sake, Terry, you stole his dog!"

"I can be very persuasive and as for Clyde, he chose us over Sawyer Brown. I didn't steal anything. Clyde! You go home," Terry ordered, looking at the mutt, furrowing his brow. The dog wagged its tail, slowly at first, then faster as it jumped forward and stood on its back legs, front paws on Terry's chest as he tried to lick the man's face. "Stop it, Clyde!" Terry pushed the dog down and scratched behind his ears. He stood next to his new human, leaning heavily against his leg.

Billy laughed. "I think he wasn't as loyal to Sawyer Brown as he thought. Let me have those two M16s. Maybe ten rounds of ammunition?"

Terry looked at what he'd collected from his people. He carried a total of twenty-seven of the 5.56mm. "Ten sounds fine. We'll be able to overwhelm anyone with all the 7.62 we recovered. I'll play sniper—one shot, one kill," Terry offered.

He walked away to be by himself, leaving Devlin with the horses, Billy and Ivan with the extra rifles. Terry looked at the mountains and breathed in the hot, dry air. He tasted the wildflowers that grew readily in the new world. Clyde followed him as he walked around what used to be a neighborhood. Only a couple houses were standing. The engineer lived in one and the mechanic in another. Billy kept his key people close.

They were the future. And they went about their job, not knowing how close they were to being on the business end of one of Sawyer Brown's pistols.

Terry thought about the engagement for the fiftieth time. He'd replay it over and over in his head until something replaced it. He couldn't help himself, because he was his own harshest critic. Without Char, they would have failed. He would have died, and the town would have fallen to a foul creature and his eight men.

Easy as that. But Char had joined them and had fought

like the devil incarnate. Was Terry lucky or good? He couldn't shake the thought that it was luck.

He also had to admit that he could trust her. She fought on behalf of the town. Had she wanted, she could have stayed in Werewolf form and killed all nine men by herself and then the entirety of the FDG, small as it was.

Then, when it was all over, she deferred to Terry.

He wasn't sure he'd been wrong about her, but for the meantime, he'd call a truce. She had earned the benefit of the doubt. "What do you think, Clyde? I'm not sure Margie Rose allows dogs in the house. We're going to have to talk her into it, so you need to be on your best behavior. Do you get me, Private Clyde?" Terry said in his Marine voice. The dog thought they were playing and bolted for the nearest stick, returning with a chunk of old two by four.

Terry relieved him of it and threw it as far as he could down the road. Clyde raced after it, the sounds of his nails on the broken pavement mixed with birds singing in the distance. At that one moment in time, everything was right with the world.

❖ ❖ ❖

"Those people didn't deserve that," Mark told Jim as they looked around the area. They found the trail where the couple's bodies had been dragged and then dumped in a ditch where the coyotes had already paid them a visit. The cabin was smoldering, nothing left of it but ash. Jim found an old shovel head with the handle mostly burned away. He got on his knees to use the shovel head to cover the bodies with dirt, giving them a more decent burial than what the raiders had given them.

When they were finished, they rode the horses slowly toward the barracks. Terry told them to water and feed the new additions to the FDG. They were mobile and both of the men appreciated not having to walk, so taking care of the mounts took on a new level of importance.

Although they suspected that Terry Henry Walton would continue to run them into the ground, since he considered physical fitness to be a critical element to the thinking warrior.

❖ ❖ ❖

When Char left the house, she was a completely changed person. She wore Billy's last pair of jeans and a button down shirt that was tied at the waist with the sleeves rolled up. Her hair was braided in a way that highlighted the silver streak. She also wore a limited amount of makeup. Felicity hugged her as she sent Char on her way. Billy watched from an upstairs window, knowing better than to get caught ogling.

Ah, the old days, when I simply took what I wanted. I kind of miss those, he thought, but then decided that if she could kill four armed men with her bare hands, she had secrets that maybe he didn't want to explore. Terry seemed completely unafraid, but by their accounts, Terry and Char faced nine men alone.

Billy couldn't fathom that.

Char saw Terry raise his eyebrows. "Shut up," she bitched. "I kind of had no choice once Felicity got started. You don't want to make her angry, and I'm sure Miss Margie Rose will appreciate the effort, so here I am." She shrugged.

"Devlin!" Terry called. "You and Ivan take two horses to your place. Make sure they get plenty of water and all the grass they can eat. They need it. I'll be by the barracks tomorrow to hear what Mark and Jim found." Terry slapped the young man on the back, gave a thumbs up to Ivan, and mounted his horse. Char climbed on hers and they rode west, slowly, each to their own thoughts. Clyde ran along happily beside them.

When they arrived home, Terry and Char hobbled the horses and turned them loose in the closest thing they had to a pasture, a large open field behind the house. It had more weeds than grass, but that was all the horses were going to get. Terry hand-pumped water into a tub and left that out back for the animals to use as they wished. When they went inside, Clyde didn't hesitate and ran inside with them.

"What was that ruckus I heard earlier, sounded like gunfire. Hey! What is that coyote doing in here? Shoo!" Margie Rose yelled as she reached for her broom. She chased after him, which he thought was great fun until Terry intercepted the older woman and asked her to sit down so he could tell her how Clyde came to join them.

Terry deposited Margie Rose on the couch as he turned a dining room chair around to sit on it backwards. Char sat next to Margie Rose, who suddenly noticed the hair and makeup. All thoughts of Clyde were relegated to the back seat. The dog whimpered until Char invited him next to her where he laid on the couch against his alpha, happy to have such a position in his new pack.

TH told the story, leaving out the parts of who killed whom, but assuring Margie Rose that she was safe. The older woman felt no fear with her Mr. Walton around.

Terry should have known.

It was late afternoon by the time Margie Rose started cooking dinner. She chased the other three outside to keep the horses from eating what flowers there were around her property. Terry and Char found that they were too late. The horses were clipping everything off right above the dirt, just like a goat would.

"I say we don't tell her," Terry suggested. Char nodded as Clyde helped them chase the horses farther from the house. They headed toward the small scrub where Terry had gotten the first couple rabbits, just in case something new appeared. As they approached, Clyde growled and dashed into the brush. There was furious barking and a real coyote was flushed out the other side with Clyde close on his tail. The coyote made a loop, outpacing the bigger dog as it headed for the two humans. Char glared at the thing and it yipped as if it had been shot, then bolted away as fast as its legs would carry it.

"Clyde!" Terry yelled to distract the dog from the fruitless chase.

With tongue lolling, he happily returned to his pack. "If there were any more rabbits in there, they are gone now. Damn coyotes. If I only had more ammunition, I'd clean those things out," Terry said absentmindedly, looking into the distance where the coyote had disappeared. Char shrugged, indifferent to the presence of coyotes. She knew that she could chase them away with just a look.

They returned to the house and after a quick wrestling match with their new furry friend, decided that he needed to stay outside while they prepared dinner and ate. He seemed to be perfectly happy ripping anything from the pan while it was cooking. As he tried to get at their dinner while it cooked on the small wood stove, Margie Rose smacked him right on his nose with her ever-present wooden spoon, and then Terry dragged the hungry beast out the front door, promising him that he'd get the leftovers. Clyde remained on the porch, waiting to come back inside.

"Let me get this straight, you show up and you're here for a few weeks, then she shows up and almost immediately a group of armed men arrive to take over the town. Tell me how the problem isn't you two?" she asked, half-kidding.

"Because we would die to protect you, Margie Rose. You won't ever have to live through a visit from the boys or anything like that again. The wastelands are calming down enough that people are able to grow what they need, find game, and venture out. That's the big difference, nothing else," Terry soothed.

He believed what he was saying. The world had settled into a new normal and people like Billy Spires were dragging the world toward a new civilization. Electrical power! Raw materials and factories. The sky was the limit.

"You're going to see a whole new world, Margie Rose, one that you're proud to be a part of," Char added, almost as if reading Terry's mind.

CHAPTER THIRTEEN

After three days of riding with his mind encased in a dark fog, Sawyer and his men entered the small town they called their own. Sawyer Brown slid from his mount and walked into his small home, shutting the door behind him. He wanted to sleep in his own bed and do it for an extended period of time.

He was happy that Terry Henry Walton didn't follow. He was in no shape to fight, no matter how much he tried to will himself into the mood. The other men had had enough riding double as well, but Sawyer didn't care about their discomfort.

The young man grabbed Sawyer's horse and didn't try to ask him about the trip. The other two men shook their heads. Jagoff drew a line across his throat with one finger. They'd wait to talk until the boss was out for the night. Which didn't take long. He was snoring inside five minutes.

In a low, conspiratorial voice, the man known as Jagoff told the others how they were ambushed by demons from Hell. How their enemy ripped the still-beating hearts from their brothers. How a stunning woman with purple eyes bested Sawyer Brown in a straight up fight in less than two seconds. Their men died quickly and even the boss fled from the battle before he joined the others in death.

Jagoff had three days to improve his tale, even growing more animated with its telling. The others in the town that Sawyer called Brownsville were fascinated, eyes widening in fear. At the end, Jagoff told them that they were going back, all of them, to face the military man and the demon woman. He told them to make peace with their makers because when they next went north, none of them would return.

Jagoff believed the last part. He knew that the boss couldn't protect any of them. He couldn't even protect himself.

❖ ❖ ❖

Terry stood in front of the barracks with his arms crossed. They'd left the horses to graze so they could continue their return to health, so he and Char had just run the distance from Margie Rose's house to the barracks. He wasn't pleased that it was taking so long for the horses. He wanted to get on the road, get after Sawyer Brown. The longer they delayed the colder the trail would get.

His people came running out as soon as Mrs. Grimes made them aware that Terry was waiting.

"Well?" Terry yelled, looking at the window where the old lady waved cordially.

"It's fine, dear," she said, but Terry wasn't having it.

"Well?" Terry repeated, this time to the four men now standing at attention. Mark shrugged. "DISHES!"

They bolted out of formation and inside, where Mrs. Grimes yelled at them to take care. Char giggled through it all.

"What are you laughing at?" he prodded.

"You. You have them jumping, but you're just a big pussy-cat," she whispered. Terry didn't understand why she was talking so low. The men inside were making enough noise, they couldn't have heard an internal combustion engine. "You shouldn't be able to hear me, but you can. Why is that?" she asked.

"Good genes. My parents were physical specimens, in the best of health. Maybe my body is made better, but it doesn't make me better," he replied, whispering as well. "And your excuse?"

"The same. Good family, that's all," she answered, her purple eyes twinkling. Terry let it go. Now wasn't the time.

Three minutes later, the four men were back outside. No one was out of breath, but they were wet. Terry walked toward the house. Mrs. Grimes waved him away. He ignored her and tried to get inside, but she blocked his way with her body. He looked over her head where he saw the table cleared and the dishes done, but there was a small lake in the kitchen that was working its way into the adjoining dining area.

"You go! Keep those brutes out of here for the next fifteen minutes. I shudder to think what this place will look like if you make them help me with that!" She pushed Terry with her small hands. She may as well have tried to move one of the Rocky Mountains.

"As you wish, Mrs. Grimes, but they shouldn't leave the house like this. You're not their slave," Terry told her.

"It's a hundred times better than it used to be," the old woman said with a smile, putting her hand on his arm gently, as a grandmother would do. "I enjoy being here. Thank you, Mr. Walton. And if it's not too much trouble, tell those goons to bring something to eat when they return home. We're getting low."

"Capital idea, Mrs. Grimes. I've been thinking a lot lately about beer. It's time. Today is the day!" Terry proclaimed, loud enough for all to hear.

"That's not what I was thinking of…" Her voice trailed off as Terry closed the door and returned to the small formation.

"First, we break down the rifles. Fifteen seconds to take them apart and forty-five seconds to put them back together. Get ready!" The men dropped to their knees and spread out a cleaning rag that they now kept with them at all times, for that very purpose. "Go!" Terry counted out loud because there were very few working watches anymore. Who knew the right time or date in order to set one?

When Terry counted to fifteen, the rifles were apart, except for Ivan's. He took two more seconds to finish. Terry pulled his bullwhip in a flash and cracked it over their heads. "What the fuck, Ivan?" Terry yelled. The man knew better than to argue. "Now put them back together on my mark. Mark." And the men put the pieces back in place, one by one, ending with snapping the upper receiver group into the lower. Even Ivan finished on time. Only Char noticed that Terry slowed his count down. She rolled her eyes at him.

The men didn't ask why she wasn't training with a weapon because it wasn't their place to ask. Terry was comfortable not giving her a weapon. If things got that bad, then she could change into a Werewolf and save herself.

"One more time!" Terry yelled. Four iterations later, he

nodded to Char with his eyebrows raised. He didn't have to slow down the count. The men were getting better. "Sling arms and next stop, the greenhouses!" The team formed, and Terry took off running with Clyde close by, easily keeping pace.

❖ ❖ ❖

"Billy dear, do I have to go?" Felicity drawled seductively. Billy knew that he was getting played, but this was what she wanted so he was going to give her a taste of her own medicine.

"Felicity, my dearest love, yes! We work for the people, not them for us. The little help we provide makes their day! And it makes mine, too. I feel more alive, more loving, more in touch with the people we need to carry us all back to the modern world, Felicity. My greatest desire is to drive a car so you can ride everywhere you want to go," he said with a smile, tenderly caressing her face.

In reality, he didn't want to be digging in the dirt alone. She was starting to understand that he learned more from her than she intended.

"Why, of course, you're right, Billy dear. How could I have not seen that?" she replied, kissing him on the cheek, but not leaning too close. He was wearing the same pants he'd been wearing for nearly a month straight. Felicity burned his other clothes and gave away his last pair of pants to Char. He only had two shirts left as well, and had taken to wearing the same one every day. She decided that her hasty actions in burning all his clothes were ill-advised, and in his way, he was making her pay for it.

Touché.

They headed into the great outdoors, turning east toward the morning sun for a cool stroll to the greenhouses and fields. The fresh air smelled good. The crispness of fall approached, even though it was still late summer. Billy felt good about the direction the town was going. He looked in the direction of the power plant, seeing the lights twinkling. He couldn't hear the hum of the natural gas-fired system, but he knew it was there.

Felicity could feel Billy's good mood and decided that she'd be in a good mood, too.

❖ ❖ ❖

Terry greeted Billy and Felicity as he and the others ran past on their way to the greenhouses. He deposited his charges one at a time at their usual places. He liked the relationships they'd built with each of the farmers, seeing that they'd become more integrated with the community. From village toughs to hard-working partners. It was amazing what a little adult leadership could do. And excising a cancer like John. *Some people just don't deserve to coexist with decent folk*, Terry thought and added, *It's not the Spanish Inquisition, just a little haircut, that's all.*

Devlin was dropped at the first greenhouse, joining his new friends, Ivan with the second, then Jim, and Mark in the fourth. Char joined Terry although he tried to drop her at the fourth greenhouse. She wasn't going there because she suspected that was where Billy and Felicity would end up. It was the largest of the five.

Terry didn't want to fight, so he quickly capitulated, plus he had an ulterior motive. Over the weeks, he'd been consolidating a variety of pots and vats for his first attempt at making beer. He needed Char to work while he played.

When they arrived, the farmers were pleased as usual and even had fresh, warm buns sweetened with wild honey. Terry liked civilization and it seemed that Char did, too. Who wouldn't when they were treated like that?

"Beer, my good man! Today is the day," Terry told Pepe Morales. His family had immigrated at some point in the past, but none of that mattered anymore. In the here and now, Terry considered Pepe to be a hero, because he selflessly grubbed in the dirt so others could eat.

Pepe grinned and slapped Terry on the back as they headed outdoors.

They had malted the barley a week prior, by taking the grain, adding water, letting it start to germinate, then removing the water and drying the barley. Pepe put a three-gallon pot of water on the fire. They needed to get the water hot, add the malted barley, and stir it together to release the starches from the grains. That process would take one to two hours, then they'd drain that, using the grain bed as the filter. Terry wanted a second sparging, as it was called, to flush as much starch from the mash as he could.

Then they'd boil the drained off liquid to reduce the water in the mixture and bring out the full flavor of what would become beer. Once that was done, they'd pour the mixture into a fermenting tank, where they'd add yeast, a rough concoction that Pepe had been working on for years with the help of his wife. Once the yeast was added, they'd put that vessel in as cool a place as possible for anywhere up to a month.

Starting today, beer in a month. Char didn't see the allure in any of it. She'd had beer before, probably even too much of it, but she never liked the taste. Of all things to bring back, she wondered why Terry wasn't working on champagne. She'd mentioned it more than once and Margie Rose concurred. A chilled bottle of champagne would be incomparable.

Terry brushed them both off with a claim that there were no grapes. Char told him she'd seen grapes in the mountains, but he wasn't convinced and even if he had been, he was not going into the mountains looking for grapes.

She assured him there was no danger, but he didn't know if that was just a lure to deliver him to the rest of the pack or what. He wouldn't risk it. No grapes and no champagne.

He told her that he was brewing the champagne of beers.

Two hours of weeding for Pepe's wife and Char, followed closely by an hour of picking ripe vegetables while the men played with the fire, keeping the mixture from boiling as they stirred and mixed. Although they were outside, the smell of the boiling wort permeated the greenhouse, completely befouling the air. Maria, Pepe's wife, went outside more than once to give a hearty what-for to the men. Char could hear her clearly railing on her husband with implications for Terry as well. The men took the tongue-lashing like champions, apologizing profusely, but they couldn't move the heated wort at that point. Live and learn. Marie cast serious doubt on whether there would be a next time.

Once she left and was out of earshot, Char could hear the two men talking. "Next time, we go downwind. Man, is this going to be good. I may have to give up my life as the security chief…" Followed by chuckles and snickers.

Char and Maria wrapped up and sat down at a small table by the front door to the greenhouse. Maria made tea from leaves that she herself had cultivated. She added thinly sliced ginger root, for a little extra kick. When the men came inside for a drink of water, they looked surprised to see that the inside work had been suspended.

"What? You two idiots stink this place up while you're playing, and you expect us to work?" Maria jabbed. Terry and Pepe were covered in sweat and reeked to high heaven. There was no doubt that they were working hard at what they were doing, but Maria believed their efforts were of no value.

"But-but..." Pepe stammered, looking longingly at the tea. Maria shook her head and pointed for him to go to the hand pump that fed their rudimentary irrigation system.

Terry watched, trying to stay out of Maria's line of sight. Char eyed him, wiggling her fingers to wave at him as she sat relaxed with her feet propped up on a rough-hewn stand, nursing her cup of tea. Terry closed his eyes. He felt like he was married, but with none of the good stuff. He couldn't share his secrets with Char, but she was always there. She needled him silently as if willing him to break or just to get a rise and have a laugh. When he opened his eyes, she was still smiling at him, then she held her nose and waved him away.

Terry walked over to the pump. "You know, Pepe, this better be the best fucking beer I've ever tasted," Terry admitted glumly.

"I'm with you there, partner," Pepe said as he tried to wash in the trickle of water that the pump delivered. The farmer stripped bare and rinsed out his clothes. Terry joined him as they wrung out their clothes, wet them, then wrung them out again. They heard voices and turned to find Maria, Char, Billy, and Felicity watching them. Pepe started to flail, but Terry stopped him.

"This is where lesser men fail, my friend," Terry told Pepe, before looking at the assembled group. Felicity ogled him appreciatively, while Char covered her mouth, trying to keep from laughing. "If you'll excuse us, we'll be out back drying our clothes. We invite you not to join us." Terry turned, sniffed a flower, grabbed a cherry tomato, and popped it in his mouth as he strolled leisurely toward the back door.

❖ ❖ ❖

Sawyer wanted to hurt somebody.

His head was still fuzzy and his eye continued to hurt. At least the swelling was finally going down. He was not up for another horse ride, although he knew he would have to make the trip. No one stood up to Sawyer Brown like that and lived to tell about it. He felt like he'd lost the respect of his men. That idiot Jagoff seemed to be a new leader among the ingrates.

"Jagoff!" Sawyer yelled from his couch. A young man entered. "I didn't call for you, Asswipe!" he bellowed.

"Sorry, boss. Jagoff is out in the field with the horses," the man pleaded from the doorway, afraid to enter.

"What the hell is he doing out there?"

"The horses have taken ill. One's dead and another is in trouble," the man replied.

"Which horses?" Sawyer asked, suspecting he knew the answer.

"The two that you returned with."

Sawyer pulled himself upright and swayed as he stood, then staggered out the door, cuffing the young man in the head as he passed. He stumbled down the road, because he wasn't able to focus clearly on the ground. A rock seemed to jump up and trip him. When he realized he was falling, it was too late. With a thud and a grunt, Sawyer Brown landed on his face in the dirt.

"That fucking bitch dies for what she did to me. I will peel the skin from her body one strip at a time," the big man swore to mother earth beneath him. "She dies... Asswipe!"

The young man helped Sawyer to his feet and as much as it pained him to ask for help, he wrapped a big arm around the other man's shoulders for support. Together they continued out of their small town and to the stable where the horses were kept. They hadn't taken that many horses in the raid into what used to be Kansas, and with the loss of the six on their ill-fated trip north, they were down to six healthy nags.

That wasn't enough to make a quick raid north. He decided that he'd take everybody on his next trip out, accepting that it would take as long as it took. Most of them would walk, but they'd get there eventually and with the full weight of his people, they'd wipe out the upstarts and take everything they owned. Purple eyes was his. She would die by his hand, slowly.

For the first time since she pounded his head, he started to think clearly. He continued to stumble along, but finally, his thoughts weren't scrambled.

That made him happy until he arrived to find that the second horse had died, too.

"Something they ate, boss. I think when we jumped off the road just after we started our return here," Jagoff told him, refusing to say the words that drove the boss into a frenzy. *After we got our asses handed to us by a girl and a guy...*

CHAPTER FOURTEEN

With the beer doing what it needed to do in a crock pot vat Terry had acquired, he and Pepe shook hands. Together, they cheered their brewing success, then went back to the real work.

For Terry, that meant collecting the boys and getting them ready to leave tomorrow on their first military expedition. They were heading out on an S&D.

A search and destroy operation.

Terry and Char walked from the greenhouse while Pepe was busy apologizing to his wife, working overtime to get back into her good graces.

Terry felt no such need with Char. At least his clothes weren't infused with barley wort. They were still moist, but he couldn't wait any longer for them to dry. "Thank you for joining the peep show. Next time, maybe a little heads up? Poor Pepe was shaken to his core."

"I saw that you weren't," she countered.

"Are you kidding me? At that moment in time, I was on top of the world. We had just brewed the first batch of beer in twenty years. I'm pretty sure that it doesn't get any better than that, plus, good Marine Corps training. Once you've lost the battle, take it with dignity and grace, then regroup for a royal ass-kicking," Terry explained.

"Is that what we're doing now, regrouping?" Char watched him closely. "May I call you TH?"

"Interesting train of thought you have. You see me naked and now you want to be friendly," he taunted her. "Yes, you may, just until I tell you you can't and please, not in front of the others. Deal?"

Char nodded, then rolled her finger, expecting the answer to her other question.

He continued looking around as they talked. "We won the first battle, so we aren't regrouping, they are. That means we are on our way to win the war. The next skirmish with these ass clowns will be their last. We're taking the fight to them, which means I'll need your help in tracking them, and Clyde's. I think he'll probably be able to lead us right to them," Terry suggested.

Char furled her brow. "Why do you think I'm good at tracking, TH?" she asked as if accusing him of slander.

"I'm a good judge of people. If you're not, that's fine. I'll admit I was wrong and we move on. No disrespect intended, Char," Terry countered.

She shook her head. "None taken," she replied. "I'll be able to help, but I think we can trust Clyde to get us there. Can't we, boy?" She ruffled the dog's head, remembering that Clyde was with them.

He had disappeared when the wort started to cook, and

showed back up when his pack left the greenhouse.

They walked for a while in silence, Terry carrying a woven bag with a small amount of vegetables. When they reached the fourth greenhouse, they collected Mark, who carried an armload of produce, after having just helped his friends load their cart for a trip to the mayor's house and to make deliveries throughout their small town.

Then they picked up Jim, finding that Billy and Felicity were there, visiting. Felicity smiled at Terry until Billy pulled on her arm.

"She'll never look at you the same way again," Char teased. Terry only shook his head, unable to make eye contact with the young woman. Terry walked away from the others and waved Billy to him.

"We're taking the horses and leaving at dawn. We'll find that motherfucker and we'll put an end to his adventurism. Then we'll look for that stash of weapons I know must be down there. Maybe that's where he got his stocks, but I don't think so. What I think is hidden would be American-made," Terry Henry told the mayor.

Billy thought about saying something sarcastic about not being given an option regarding whether the FDG left or not, but they'd already decided after Sawyer Brown's attack that Terry was going to take the battle to them. He thought about trying to come up with a motivational speech, but Terry probably would think it condescending. He settled for something simple. "Good luck," Billy said, holding out his hand. Terry shook it, then waved at Char as he headed down the road.

❖ ❖ ❖

Sawyer was feeling stronger with each new day. He walked by himself, albeit slowly, but at least the ground didn't move anymore when he walked over it. The only thing he thought about during the walks was what he would do to Purple Eyes after he watched his men gun down Terry Henry Walton. Maybe he'd start by shooting her kneecaps so she couldn't jump in his face. Then she'd be at his mercy. He'd start by removing her clothes quickly, but then he'd remove her skin slowly. Starting with her back and working his way forward. He could hear her screams in his mind as she begged him to stop, as she pleaded with him for mercy, that she'd do anything for him if he'd make the pain go away.

"Yes, my pretty, we'll make the pain go away, in the end, after you've put up with as much of it as you can't believe you can tolerate. Slowly, my pretty. Perfection can't be rushed," he talked out loud.

No one was nearby as he continued to hear her screams. *Yes, more of that*, he thought.

Jagoff had no idea what killed the horses, but the six remaining were getting special treatment, extra grass, rub-downs, and anything the men could think of to keep them happy and healthy. The horses were filling out with the extra food, and Sawyer saw the wisdom in that. The horses were too weak on their last trip to give them the advantage of speed. For round two, he wanted to ride in fast, use the boys' superior firepower to flood the area with bullets. Everyone needed to just die, except for Purple Eyes and any other woman they found. Sawyer wanted a cook and a plaything. He expected that there would be plenty of those in that town of theirs. They would do anything to have their miserable lives saved, just like in the first days following the fall.

Sawyer had taken advantage of people in that time, but

then he'd given them his protection, too. Not an insignificant thing in a world without a civilized society.

Just until he grew tired of them, then he'd turn them over to his boys when the next one came along. Then they stopped coming, and he had to find new sources for his depredations.

It had been a long time since they'd found a new woman. That made Sawyer perpetually angry. His head felt better, but that only led him down fury road, where the only thing that mattered was revenge and taking it out on the world around him. Sharing his pain was the only way he had of dealing with it.

And he was okay with that.

"When can we go, you fucking morons?" Sawyer yelled at the men in the stables brushing the horses. Jagoff appeared, wearing a big, forced smile.

"Any day now, boss. Any day! We've got some hooves that we're dealing with but as soon as we find something we can use for shoes, we'll be ready and get going. Give me three days?" Jagoff asked.

"You have two, fuckstick," Sawyer answered. That was all Jagoff wanted. He knew how the game was played and set it up perfectly for his boss.

"The morning of the third day from now, we'll ride out. What do you need from me, boss?" the man asked.

"Everyone goes. Get them all ready. No one remains behind. Tell them to lube up their walking shoes."

❖ ❖ ❖

Dawn found the FDG on the road where they had engaged Sawyer Brown's mob a week prior. It was the most convenient starting point between the barracks and Margie Rose's home.

MARTELLE AND ANDERLE

They each rode easily. Six of them, all armed, saddlebags filled with food and ammunition.

Mrs. Grimes and Margie Rose had gone overboard preparing meals for their warriors. Terry almost felt guilty, but the food was so good that he couldn't turn it down. He felt like he was taking the team out on a picnic. From the looks on their faces, it was hard to believe that wasn't the case.

TH turned his horse around to face the men, not an easy feat since he was still teaching himself how to ride.

"Listen up. That last battle did not test our mettle. We surprised them. We won't have that advantage next time. I expect they'll shoot on sight, so what do we need to do, people?" Terry looked for someone to answer. Mark waved a hand.

"We see them first," he said simply.

"Exactly, we see them first. The hard question is, how do we do that?" Terry looked from face to face in the dim light of early dawn.

"We spread out. Hunt alone," Char suggested, looking south, into the distance where her quarry was.

"Hunt. Yes, we're hunting them. We keep our distance, don't get bunched up, stay within sight of one another, and keep quiet. We move like the wind in the grass. Understand?" A chorus of "yes, sir" followed. Then Terry went through a quick series of hand and arm signals, so they could "talk" as long as they could see each other. For the first half of the journey, Terry and Char would take the lead, riding in pairs, a couple hundred yards between the first group and the second and then another between second and the third. Further, each would ride toward a side of the road. Separation for safety's sake and situational awareness were key for a combat movement, which Terry considered this to be.

He and Char headed out, riding as far apart as possible while still being on the same road. Then Devlin and Ivan, and bringing up the rear were Mark and Jim. Everyone had a role to play.

"I think I'd like a weapon," Char said conversationally from the other side of the road.

"The next one we acquire is yours," Terry replied in a soft, even tone. He didn't commit to giving her any ammunition. That would be a different conversation for a different day.

"No, that's not it. I think I want Sawyer Brown's pistols, both of them. You called them Glocks?" she asked.

"Yes, Glock. At least the one I saw was. Glock was one of many manufacturers of firearms, but their specialty was pistols. This baby here—" Terry patted the hand cannon at his side. "—was made by Colt and it has been around for a while. It could be a hundred years old, who knows, but the design is classic. It succeeded in the trial of combat and was the preferred weapon of the Corps. It's my honor to carry one again," Terry said reverently.

"Honor. The Corps. Classic. What kind of words are those, TH? Who talks like that anymore?" she asked, wondering about the strange man. "As a young girl, I remember hearing stories with the Knights of the Round Table. Is that you, Terry Henry Walton? Are you a Knight of Camelot?"

Terry wondered at her age. Of course she would look young, no matter how old she was. He was in his sixties and looked to be thirty. Could she be one hundred? He had no idea, but couldn't imagine anyone hearing stories about the Knights of the Round Table in the time following the World's Worst Day Ever.

"Once a Marine, always a Marine. To me, there's nothing more important than personal honor. At the end of the day, when it's just you in that foxhole, it's the only thing that will keep you going. When the fight's over and you look yourself in the mirror, you want to see the honorable person looking back at you. Otherwise life is too hard." Terry watched the mountains as he let his horse set a pace it was comfortable with. He rubbed its neck constantly, letting the mare know that he appreciated the ride.

Char used her keen eyes to look far in front. "How much venison did you bring?" she asked, knowing that she didn't have enough. She ate an unnatural amount of food, most of it meat, because of her metabolism. The she-wolf within screamed for energy. She thought she was losing weight, never a good thing as a Werewolf.

"I'd like to hunt," she told TH. "All by myself, I need to go hunting. There's something wrong with me that I have to do it that way, but there you are. When we stop for the evening, I'm pleading with you." Char looked at Terry for confirmation.

Because you're a fucking Werewolf, he thought. He hoped that she would tell him the truth of her nature, but she hadn't. He wouldn't share that nanocytes coursed through his body, but he was sure she noticed he didn't have a single scar on a body hardened in the fires of the Marine Corps, in private security, and then twenty years in the wasteland.

She had to have seen that, as he'd seen her perfect body, not a scar or mark of any sort. The wasteland was never so kind to humanity. She knew he was different and he wouldn't tell her why. He knew she was different, but she wouldn't tell him, either. It was a stalemate of sorts, even though he was growing more comfortable with her.

And that scared him. He still wasn't sure why she was with the humans. Had she been expelled from the pack? That seemed odd since she arrived in perfect health. He'd have to think more on that and try to figure out a way to ask her without addressing her true nature.

That was the rest of the day, watching and riding in silence, taking breaks anytime they were close to water to let the horses drink and graze.

Terry estimated they made it twenty-five miles. That wasn't enough. They needed to go fifty tomorrow as they swung far to the east to get around the ruins of Denver, and then the next day they could start thinking about the tactical approach to the area south of Denver. Terry hoped he'd find tracks or some way to limit their search area.

❖ ❖ ❖

Gathering the people wasn't as easy as Sawyer Brown had thought it would be. There were some forty total, only six women and a couple small children. It was a pathetic bunch that prepared to travel. They weren't leaving for another full day, but already Sawyer saw that they would slow him down and significantly so.

"Jagoff!" Sawyer yelled. His new number one man ran out of a group and angled toward him.

"Yes, boss?" he yelled as he slowed to a stop, just beyond arm's reach. Sawyer brushed off the man's hesitation.

"We can't take all these stupid fuckers with us, can we?" he growled.

Jagoff was torn. He'd seen men beaten for telling the boss the truth. He'd been beaten for less. He parsed his words carefully. "We can, but only if you're willing to travel ten miles a day, maybe only five. We'd be on the road for two weeks just to get there, probably longer because we'll run out of provisions well before that time. We'll have to stop and hunt, scour the countryside for things to eat." Jagoff watched the boss carefully, ready to dodge if necessary.

"I think you're right. Split them up. I only want people that can walk twenty-five miles a day. We'll be on the road what, four days? We can carry what we need on the horses. Go." Jagoff was surprised by the matter-of-fact approach that seemed to be logic-based, so unlike the boss. But he hesitated too long and brought out the real Sawyer Brown.

A massive paw reached out and grabbed Jagoff by the collar and threw him to the ground where Sawyer kicked him in the chest. "What the fuck are you waiting for? Now fuck off and take care of it!" Sawyer lifted Jagoff to his feet and backhanded him across the face for good measure.

There was no way Jagoff was going to ask Sawyer Brown what he needed as a minimum number of people. Jagoff ran away from the big man, realized he was going in the wrong direction, then looped back toward the people who were gathering all their personal belongings for a trip into the wastelands to go someplace that was supposed to be overgrown with food and thick with game to hunt. No one believed any of that.

They looked like they were preparing to march to their deaths. The only thing missing was a funeral dirge.

Jagoff was happy that he could share some good news with them, but anyone on the fence of being able to walk for twelve solid hours each day would have to go. Sawyer wanted numbers, but very few people were healthy enough to do as he asked. Jagoff looked at the crowd and waved everyone to him. He could see Sawyer Brown over the tops of their heads as he watched to see Jagoff in action, probably wanting him to fail so he could beat him again.

That shit was getting real old.

❖ ❖ ❖

Terry pushed the group hard the second day, where they traveled single file with a hundred yards between each. He put the unarmed Char at the back of the line while he stayed up front. Terry urged his horse into a trot for fifteen minutes per hour as they traveled. They still stopped every couple hours, but as dusk approached on the second day, they'd passed Denver and were turning west to canvass the approach toward the nebulous south where Sawyer said they were from.

Even Clyde was dogged that second day, so Terry took pity and carried him on the horse for half the time.

TH didn't put great stock in the big man's claims, but it was the only thing he had. If they'd come from the east, from Kansas, then he'd never find them. The broad expanse of the wasteland was too much for a search and destroy mission. He wanted to head south anyway, find Falcon Air Force Base, find Peterson Field, see if any of NORAD remained. Those bases had to have a secret stash. Maybe even the Air Force Academy. The cadets trained with rifles. He wondered if they had a storeroom of M1 Garands, but the barrels were probably plugged. He needed weapons and ammunition he could use.

They made a small fire in a ditch because they found dry wood that wouldn't smoke. They made a stew with things they'd brought, but Char asked if she could head into the wilds to go hunting. She thought she smelled a wild boar, but no one else smelled anything. Terry pulled a knife from a leg scabbard, he flipped it over and holding it by the blade, handed it to Char. She didn't need it, but took it to maintain appearances.

She disappeared into the twilight.

"What the hell was that?" Mark asked in a low voice. "She's going out to hunt a wild boar with a little blade. In the dark. After we've ridden all day and are exhausted. What is with her? Nothing fazes that woman."

Terry looked to the three men arrayed around the small fire. Ivan was currently at the observation post they'd established, about one hundred yards away, so he could guarantee no one surprised them. Terry made sure they understood what security was all about, what it meant to participate in a real military operation.

"Gentlemen, she's the best natural hunter in this whole group. She learned when she was on her own and honed her skill. Don't let her looks fool you. She's as deadly as anyone you can imagine. She's going to go hunt and she will probably bring back the rest of her kill for us mere mortals. And you know what we're going to do? We're going to thank her and move on."

"I'd like to move on her, alright," Devlin snickered. Terry vaulted across the fire, hitting the young man in the chest with both feet. Devlin rolled over backwards as Terry straddled him, one hand wrapped around his throat and the other balled into a fist. The young man flailed his arms and winced, expecting the blow.

"You will never talk about her like that. Do you understand me?" Terry growled. He'd seen too many Marines in his day who thought they were superior to women just because they were men. He had thought that way at one point, until he learned that everyone brought unique skills to the table. And nothing would tear a unit apart more quickly than men posturing to bed a lone female.

"She is an equal member of the FDG and that's all there is to it. Who cares what she looks like? She saved my ass out there. I live because she fought the raiders. That makes her all right in my book. That makes her a warrior. And that's all there is to it. I catch any of you thinking those thoughts again, I will beat you within an inch of your life and you'll be kicked out of the Force."

Terry's voice finished, "Period fucking dot!"

"Yes, sir," Devlin gasped as Terry and got off him. "I'm sorry, I didn't mean anything by it." Terry glared at the young man beneath him.

"If you don't mean anything by it, then don't say it. Words are all we have. Words show our intent, and then our intent becomes our actions. Be proud that she's on our side, because if she ever turned, you can kiss your asses goodbye. She would kill all of you without hesitation and walk away from the fight without a scratch. You've all seen her body. You know what's important to see? Not a scratch. How in the hell do you survive in the wastelands and not get a scratch? Because you're better than everyone else, tougher than anything out there. Trust her and respect her and we'll see you through this."

Terry offered his hand to help Devlin up. The young man couldn't look into Terry's eyes. No one wanted to be made an example of, and that was where he was. The poster child of getting it wrong. Terry tipped the man's chin up. "Control your thoughts, control your actions, and you'll do right by me, by all of us," he encouraged.

Devlin nodded. Clyde started howling at the darkness until Terry yelled at him to be quiet and pulled him close as he stretched out to sleep. He had the midnight watch and that time would come too soon.

❖ ❖ ❖

Charumati hadn't gone far from the fire when she carefully removed her clothes and piled them neatly behind a rock. She changed into her Werewolf form, reveling in the power it gave her. She heard what Devlin said, and then recognized the sound of a fight. She wondered if they would feel the same way if they saw her as she was now.

She appreciated Terry coming to her defense, and that he did it as an equal and not as an alpha protecting its mate. With those thoughts to comfort her, she bolted into the near darkness, running toward the smell of her prey.

She stopped as the scent became stronger. She crouched and listened, feeling the aura of the world around her, enjoying her Were senses fully. Not far, the warmth of a mammal, the sound of it digging in the dirt. With her back legs under her, she launched herself forward and drove her sleek brown body across the tops of the rolling terrain. The distance between her and her prey disappeared under great, ground-eating strides. With a final leap, she pounced on a small javelina, a wild pig. She seized its throat in her powerful jaws, savoring the warm blood as it gushed into her mouth.

The javelina fought a losing battle from the start, guaranteeing that it would be over quickly. With most of its blood drained, Char shook the creature harshly, breaking its neck to finish the kill. She dug into it, gorging on the meat, bones, and entrails. When she finished, the skull and some of the bigger bones remained. She laid down, with the javelina skull between her front paws, and licked and nipped to get every last bit of anything edible.

She heard it at the last second. Slithering on the hard ground, slipping through soft sand. She vaulted straight into the air as the rattler struck. Its fangs grazed her back leg. The fire! She landed and bolted to give herself space, turning to face this new enemy.

It burned! Her leg was starting to stiffen, but she'd just eaten and the healing had already started.

The snake coiled, head hovering and tail rattling, ready to strike. She feigned with a paw, encouraging it to strike. A little closer. It dove. She pulled that paw and slapped the other on the back of the thing's head. She held it down as the rest of its body coiled, seeking to leverage itself free of her grip. She had no stomach to play with the thing. She bit down on the meaty part next to her paw, clamping her jaws tightly and shaking with fury that ended by tearing the snake in two pieces.

The poison's fire smoldered, no longer flames licking into her body. Her leg was loosening up as the she-wolf fought the poison.

She picked up the bulk of the snake in her mouth and trotted back the way she'd come, following her own trail by the scent she'd left. When she arrived at her clothes, she changed into her human form. The scrape from the snake's fangs were gone, and the evil of its poison was almost completely cleansed from her body. Char dressed, picked up the snake, and strolled back into camp.

Terry roused as Clyde's tail pounded him with joy at seeing his alpha. She stroked the mutt's fur, then scratched behind his ears and around his neck. Char had never considered owning a pet, least of all a dog, but here she was, and she liked it. Clyde asked for so little in return. In that way, he was like Terry Henry Walton. The two mutts of her new pack. She smiled to herself.

When Terry opened his eyes, he saw the remains of the fat rattler. He sat up and took it from her. He held out his hand for his knife, which she'd forgotten about. When he had it, he started to gut and skin the snake.

"You didn't do a very good job cutting the head off. Was my knife really that dull?" Terry asked pointedly.

"Ohhh," Char started. "It was dark," she countered. He shook his head and removed the part where the Werewolf had bitten through it and then he cut another section away from that. What would Werewolf saliva do to his people? He didn't want to find out. He threw those bits in the fire before anyone could make the mistake of trying them.

He skinned the snake, keeping the skin, knowing that he'd be able to make something out of that later, maybe even wrap the handle of his bullwhip. He cut the rattler into smaller pieces and threw that into the remainder of the dinner stew. He added more water and dusted sage into it. Sagebrush seemed to be the single item one could find anywhere throughout the wasteland.

Terry looked forward to eating a little more. He'd skimped on dinner, as had the others. Ivan said that he could probably cover the entire night, although Mark was ready to take the post whenever Nightwatch woke him. Devlin and Jim were equally ready.

Mark lifted his head when Terry added a few sticks to the fire and it burst back to life. The new concoction didn't smell great, but food was food when traveling through the wasteland.

Char snuggled next to Clyde and quickly fell asleep. Terry saw that she was halfway onto his blanket and that Clyde took the rest of it.

Just like being married, he thought. He really wanted that blanket as he knew the night would be cool. At this altitude it was almost always cool in the evening. Once he and

Mark ate their fill, he kicked dirt over the fire to put it out, then wrapped himself around Clyde, letting the dog provide warmth. He soon found that Char was generating more heat than Clyde. That should not have surprised him, but it did.

He got close enough so that he felt like he was sleeping in front of a fire, hugging a bear rug to him.

To Mark, it looked like Clyde, Terry, and Char were intertwined as a single being. He thought about it, jealous for only a moment, then envious, before finally realizing that it didn't matter. She was her own person and could choose who she spent time with. He trusted Terry and Terry trusted her. Easy as that.

CHAPTER FIFTEEN

Sawyer sat on his horse, feeling like his old self. His head was clear and his body responded to his demands. It had been a couple weeks since the bitch had hit him in the head, and now that he could think clearly, he couldn't remember what she hit him with. He thought it was just her hand, but that was impossible. He convinced himself that she'd been wearing brass knuckles.

It was the only answer that made any sense to him. His eye socket was tender to the touch, so he kept his fingers away. He rode on their best horse, happy that his people had seen that was the only option. Jagoff was on a horse, as were four others. The rest were walking. It hurt the man to see those miserable souls pack their meager belongings together so that the five men on horseback could carry their goods. Sawyer carried nothing extra, but he was heavier than any two of the other men.

Sawyer led the way, setting a pace that made those on foot run. Some in the back were walking and the ones up front were running as much as they could. All it did was spread the fifteen out across a long distance. Fifteen men struggled to keep up.

Sawyer continued to ride ahead, feeling that they'd catch up if they wanted to eat. All their food was on the horses. Jagoff tried to stay with the people, but he knew that wouldn't work because Sawyer would flip out. He told the walkers he was sorry and waved goodbye.

Jagoff galloped ahead until he caught up with the others on horseback. Sawyer glared back at him, then waved him forward. The man exhaled deeply, still feeling the pain from his last beating. His rifle was so close. He could end it, but Sawyer Brown provided for him when he was dying, and he continued to provide for the mass of humanity that gathered around him. If his only deprivation was to hit and kick people, it was a small price to pay for life.

Trying to hold that thought in mind, he rode even with the big man. "What's up, boss?" he asked guardedly.

"I thought we'd lose those lazy fuckers. That was always a gamble, but we can't afford to wait. We'll continue to ride ahead, rifles at the ready. We shoot first and ask questions later. Pass it to the men and then get back there and tell those stupid bastards to hurry up. They don't want to fall too far behind. They'll get lost in the wasteland and then no one will be able to save them, not even me," Sawyer growled.

Jagoff tipped his head and rode back down the line. "Rifles loaded and at the ready, boys. We're hunting assholes, and they are in season. Shoot first, ask questions later. Ride in pairs, you knuckleheads, so one of you can watch right and the other left." He waved dismissively at them before spurring his mount back to the walkers.

He pulled his horse up short and waited for the first man to arrive. A younger man was breathing heavily, when he ran up and stopped, leaning on Jagoff's horse. "Do your best to help the others find their way. I'll leave a trail for you, mark the ground if we make a turn, so you know which way we went. The boss is pressing forward. I don't think he's going to wait, but you have to catch up to us if you want to eat."

Jagoff looked up the road and saw that Sawyer Brown had disappeared around a corner. Jagoff took his saddlebags off and slid them down to the man. "I hope it's enough food for the group for a couple days at least. Spread it around and do your best," he told the man. Jagoff nodded and spurred his horse forward. He hung on as the beast galloped down the road, its ad hoc shoes clanging oddly as each hoof hit the ground.

When he caught up with the others, he stayed in the back by himself, magazine inserted in his AK47 and barrel pointed skyward so he could shift it right or left more quickly. The others faced their rifles outboard, toward the fields and scrub on either side of the road. Sawyer rode in the front, sullen but alert. His head turned back and forth as he incessantly scanned the horizon. Jagoff had never seen the boss afraid like this.

Sawyer Brown was dangerous when he acted like he didn't care, but Jagoff wondered what he could unleash when the big man was singularly focused on revenge.

❖ ❖ ❖

"It's getting cold early this year, Marcus," Ted said, trying to get in the alpha's good graces.

Ted didn't understand that inane small talk wasn't the way to impress the great wolf that led them.

"Fuck off," Marcus had replied.

He glowered from the woods toward a small valley, high between a couple perpetually snow-covered Rocky Mountain peaks. Elk grazed peacefully, unaware that at that moment, seven Werewolves stalked them. Marcus had ordered the pack to take them all. Four she-wolves and three of the males were inching toward the open ground. On command, they'd bolt into the small herd together.

The goal was no less than one kill each. Marcus delivered his expectation to the pack and turned them loose. The Werewolves usually hunted elk in pairs, but he wanted to send a message to his wolves. By doing his bidding, the others would have to raise their game.

Tim slinked away, hoping to join the others, maybe even make a kill of his own. Only actions impressed Marcus. There were no words that could change his mind.

He did not think kindly of Tim. Although Marcus had called Tim a twatwaffle, he thought better of him than that, but not much. Those were only words. Marcus watched the Werewolves break cover as one and flow across the field, each selecting a single elk as their prey.

With a good hunt, maybe they'd return early and see what kind of progress Char made in infiltrating the human village. He wasn't sure he liked it, but the taste of human called to him, a forbidden fruit, a magical elixir that turned him into a dark and brooding master of the Were world.

Maybe the Forsaken would see him in a new light. He could only hope.

❖ ❖ ❖

When Sawyer finally stopped for the evening, he'd gone far beyond anything the walkers were going to manage. He made the men spread out, and ordered that they eat their food cold because he wouldn't allow any fires. Jagoff felt as if they were going to war like real soldiers.

Sawyer Brown continued to brood over the situation. There were only six of them riding far in front of the other fifteen. He could set up and wait, or continue to press forward. Once he found his enemy, he planned on ambushing them. Sawyer was under no illusion that he was in the weaker position. It was also not beneath him to shoot a man in the back, or a woman for that matter. All he had to do was find them before they found him.

When the horses were hobbled in an old field and the men set in a good hundred yards away, Sawyer thought he heard a familiar howl.

At that point he knew.

He walked carefully from one man to the next. "Be ready, sleep in shifts," he told them. "These fuckers are like the night wind. They will show up without a sound and then you die. There is no in between."

The men looked terrified, but Sawyer growled at them, angry at their fear, while his own tormented him. "I'm not telling you this so you can be afraid, dumbasses! I'm telling you this so when you see them, you can know that you've prepared yourselves to beat them. We will ambush them, and we will kill them all. Once you've seen the first person fall, you'll feel the power you carry. You'll feel what it's like to be me. So be ready and when we see them, we don't hesitate. We pull them in and we unload on them. Spare no ammunition. Light 'em up and watch 'em die!"

Sawyer smiled. His attempt at motivating his men was working to improve his own attitude. He slapped a couple of the men on the back and nodded to them. From one to the next, he made them look him in the eye. When he finished, he walked tall with swagger as he headed back to his own position in a culvert to the side of the old, broken road they traveled.

The big man settled in to his own thoughts as he crouched, only the top of his head sticking out over the edge of a small berm. He looked for silhouettes, for movement from an enemy he was convinced was doing the same thing that he was doing. If they didn't see them on the way, then his men would be more than ready when they reached the town. All they'd have to do was hide and wait. That man called Terry Henry and Purple Eyes would show themselves. He'd finish them, and everyone else.

The whole world would learn what it was like when you pissed on a man like Sawyer Brown.

❖ ❖ ❖

Terry Henry woke up in the middle of the night to check on his people. He had to extricate his sweat-covered arm from Char. Clyde woke up too, and followed Terry as he carefully made his way to the observation post. He found Ivan wide awake.

He'd heard Terry and Clyde approaching, confirmed that it was them, and returned watching to the south and west.

"I don't how you do it, Nightwatch, but the others will thank you greatly for a full night's sleep. You going to be able to sleep on your horse?" Terry asked.

"Are you kidding? I spent half the day today asleep in the saddle. I feel great, Mr. Walton, and thanks for giving me a chance," Ivan said in a low voice.

Terry looked at the man, still overweight, although not as much as before. "We all bring something to the game. I'd like to think that all anyone needs is a chance and someone to believe in them. Don't think that means I'll take it easy on you, either. We're in a hard business. If we fail, people die. So we train, harder and harder, so we don't lose, ever. You know the difference between an amateur and a professional, Nightwatch?" Terry asked.

Ivan turned his head and pursed his lips before answering. "I don't know, sir."

"Amateurs practice until they get it right. Professionals practice until they can't get it wrong. Which one do you think we are?"

"We can't afford to get it wrong, because then people die. I get you. These knuckleheads don't stand a chance," Ivan said confidently, louder than he intended.

"Don't get cocky, Nightwatch." Terry gripped the man's shoulder, happy to have him on board. "It's okay to wake up one of the others and get some shut-eye. We don't want our folks getting lazy, now do we?"

Terry took Clyde into the scrub so they could relieve themselves, then they returned to their camp. The others hadn't moved, except for Char.

She was nowhere to be seen.

❖ ❖ ❖

"What gives, Billy dear? Come back to bed," Felicity called from underneath a thick comforter. Billy stood at the window, wrapped in a thin blanket. He looked south, always south, because that was where the enemy had come from. That was where his security chief had gone with all his people.

That left Billy Spires to hold down the fort on his own.

If Terry didn't stop them, Billy would be almost powerless. A few weapons, almost no ammunition. And just him.

Everyone else worked. No one could stand guard if people wanted to eat, if people wanted fresh water, firewood for the winter. So much to do, and so few people to do it. Billy Spires thought about the hundred or so people who called New Boulder home. It wasn't that many, fewer than a number of years ago, but they hadn't lost anyone recently.

Besides that dickhead John. Terry killed him and the whole world seemed to be a better place. With Char, they added two and lost one. A net gain.

Char. What a magnificent creature she was. Billy couldn't figure her out. She would flirt, but she was stone cold, too. She had eyes only for Terry Henry Walton, he was convinced of that.

Who wouldn't?

Even Billy thought Terry was a Roman God. Where had these people come from? The wastelands weren't kind and here, in the course of only a few weeks, two beautiful people appeared. The wastelands belched out refuse, not the best that mankind had to offer.

"What the fuck?" Billy said.

"Watch your mouth, Billy dear," Felicity mumbled, half asleep.

"What's up with those people? Did they just take off, leave us high and dry, or are they actually out there, protecting us?" the mayor asked the darkness of the night.

The only doubt he carried was in the stories his own mind told him. He'd never met a man of honor before, but that was all Terry Henry Walton had ever shown him. He said what he was going to do, and then he did it. That was how someone demonstrated they could be trusted.

It was as simple as that.

"You better fucking win, Terry. Don't make me have to train another security guy. We just got you tightened up..."

MARTELLE AND ANDERLE

❖ ❖ ❖

False dawn drove the cold to the ground as light started to appear in the east. Sawyer Brown was already standing, holding his horse, watching. No one had seen him recover the beast from the nearby field. The others hurried after their own mounts as soon as Jagoff woke them and kicked them in the pants. They all turned when they heard footsteps. A couple men fumbled with their rifles, but Jagoff waved at them to put their weapons away.

The walkers had arrived.

The lead man had rallied the group and they walked for four hours and rested for two throughout the remainder of the day and the night. A couple people limped, but most looked no worse for wear. Sawyer showed a toothy grin when he saw the others arrive. He'd left them to their own devices, and they'd come through.

He was becoming a good leader that the people followed willingly. He climbed on his horse and rode to meet the people.

"Well done," he told them, without preamble or further explanation. He turned and let his horse stroll forward, but stopped almost immediately, holding a hand up for silence.

They all looked at the big man in shock. "There is no higher praise in the land," Jagoff whispered into the young man's ear. He thrust a fist in the air, pumping it as Jagoff ran toward the field to collect his ride.

The other mounted men had missed the exchange and sat, waiting to follow their boss up the road. Jagoff climbed into the saddle and waved at the walkers one more time as he turned his attention to the statue ahead that was Sawyer Brown.

❖ ❖ ❖

"Char! Where the hell are you?" Terry called in a rough whisper. No answer. He climbed from the low ground they were sheltered in, stood on a mound, and looked around. He saw nothing. "Char? Char!" he said in an almost normal voice.

"I heard you the first seven times, crazy man," she whispered from not far away. Terry put his hands on his hips and glared at her. "Can't a woman visit the facilities in peace without some man thinking she needs to be protected?" she asked pointedly as she strolled toward him. He walked toward her, angry that she left without his knowing.

Why was he so upset? Did he think she was going to abandon them? Was he counting on her so much that he didn't think he could do this alone? He struggled with the questions that pounded the inside of his skull. "I care. I care about you and the others all the same. I was surprised, and I don't like surprises."

"Don't I know that," she answered, putting a gentle hand on his arm as she looked into his face for a moment, then she returned to the area around the fire pit. She used a flint to restart the fire. As it burned anew, she rolled her blanket and put on a small kettle with water. She had gained a taste for the herb concoction that took the place of coffee in their new world.

Terry checked the sky, false dawn. It wasn't the middle of the night as he'd thought earlier. It was almost morning. *That damn she-wolf is messing with my head*, he thought. He had to admit that he slept soundly, more soundly and for longer than he had in forever.

With a Werewolf sleeping inches from him.

It made no sense, but he laughed it off. He was well rested and knew that today was going to be a good day.

❖ ❖ ❖

"Get down, you fucking idiots!" Sawyer whispered harshly, cupping his mouth to keep the sound focused behind him. He'd seen a man outlined against the morning sun in the waste to the east, not far off the road they were traveling.

He slowly climbed from his horse and told the others to get down without making any noise. They tried to comply, but the horses' shoes clopped on the road's surface. "Get those nags off the road," he growled. His patience was at its end.

His men led their horses into the field where they turned them loose. Sawyer crouched as he moved along the ditch, waving the others to him. When they gathered around, Sawyer noticed that a few of the walkers were there, too. "I think they are just up ahead. I need half of you to go right, set up at an angle facing toward the road, and half of you to go left. I'll stay right in the middle here because I want to pull the trigger and spring the trap. And then you people kill everything that moves."

The boss emphasized his point by drawing a finger across his throat. He waved a meaty arm to one side then the other. "Get in position, hide yourselves, and wait for my signal. Now go!" he whispered roughly. The men made more noise than he wanted as they moved away from the road and into the adjoining scrub. Ten people faded into the darkness along each side.

How in the hell did he know? All this time, I thought he was just a big goon, but the man's got skills. Damn! He knew they were close. We're going to get us some for sure! Jagoff said to himself in amazement. He went to the end of the line of people after placing them into position behind mounds or stumps. He anchored the line and settled in to wait, his new confidence in the boss giving him comfort.

Sawyer breathed deeply of the morning air. It was still dark, but the sun would rise soon. A slight breeze blew from west to east, which would mask the sounds and smells of his men. He thought he could smell smoke, and saw brief shadows cast by the pale light of a small campfire hidden behind a small mound.

Sawyer crouched in the ditch, pulled a hard roll from his pack, and chewed on it as he smiled to himself.

Am I lucky or good? he wondered. *I'm not just good, I'm fucking great!* he told himself as he settled in to wait.

CHAPTER SIXTEEN

Nightwatch scampered up to Terry, anxious and out of breath. "I think I saw something. Men on horses, but then it all melted back into the darkness. I thought I heard something, too, but with the wind, I couldn't tell," he managed to stumble through the words.

Terry kicked dirt into the fire, and the area was plunged into darkness. Their night vision was jacked from the light, so Terry and his people stood still, willing their eyes to quickly adjust.

After a few moments, both Terry and Char had recovered. He pulled her close to him and whispered in her ear. "Can you go out there, in the dark, quickly, scout the area, find them, how many and where, and return before it gets light?"

"Yes," she breathed, not even as loud as a whisper as her lips brushed against his ear, her breath hot against his skin.

She backed away soundlessly and disappeared over the hill into the darkness.

Terry pulled the men together and sat them in a tight circle. He exhaled most of the air before he started to speak, using the trick he'd been taught in the Corps. "Char's gone out to scout. Check your weapons, gentlemen. When she gets back, we'll develop our plan and we'll go, try to get into position before it gets too light. When we can, we'll take the battle to them. This is what we've been training for.

"Knuckle down and control yourselves. This is an exercise in military discipline. Sight alignment and sight picture do not change just because the target is a person. When you wade into battle, don't think about anything other than exploiting your enemy's weakness. You must kill him before he kills you. That's it. That's all there is to combat. Any questions?"

Terry knew he was rambling, but his men weren't ready for this. He didn't know what to tell them that would help to keep them alive. All he could do was keep their morale up, keep them motivated to fight with reckless abandon. It had been the tried and true technique of young Marines since the dawn of time.

If Sawyer Brown and his people were out there, the FDG would have the fight of their lives. Personally, Terry knew that he couldn't let the big man escape this time, although he suspected that Char had Sawyer's number. He'd seen the look in her eyes when they talked. She was furious that she hadn't killed him when she first had the chance.

Terry wondered when she'd return.

❖ ❖ ❖

Char moved quietly away from the camp, started undressing and then decided she'd do it as a human. If she got into the middle of a shitstorm, she'd change and take care of business. In the interim, she'd recon the old-fashioned way.

She moved at an angle away from where Ivan said he'd seen people. She moved one hundred, two hundred, four hundred yards ahead, then a half-mile. She crouched and waited. Dawn was coming.

She assumed that not being discovered was more important than hurrying, so she settled in. She could smell the campfire, even this far away, the scent of the herb and tea mixture. The musk of unwashed men, which was nowhere near as bad as wet Werewolf. It didn't bother her. The wind prevented her from smelling anything that was ahead.

She watched and finally it was light enough for her to see movement. At regular intervals, heads popped up, scanned the area, then disappeared. She counted to six, but the spacing suggested there would be more. They had set up in a line and were waiting. She disappeared into a dip and continued to angle away from the people she'd seen. If she could work her way in behind them, then she could learn everything they needed to know, like how many and what were they armed with.

Char stayed low and moved quickly. She was no more than the light breeze that whipped above her. Then she turned as she was well past the last head she'd seen. She moved from behind a low mound and froze. Twenty feet away was a man peering into the darkness. She was beyond his peripheral vision, but remained frozen and agonizingly slowly, lowered herself to the ground. She never blinked as her eyes remained fixed on her target.

She backed away on all fours, behind the mound, then

moved away without a sound, to the southeast, to put as much distance as possible between her and the man on the far right of their line before she returned to the others to report what she'd found.

The sun tipped over the horizon and light spread across the fields and rough terrain. Char felt like she'd failed.

❖ ❖ ❖

Terry tried to judge the distance in the darkness but had no luck. He watched and waited, but patience when a battle was coming was not his strong suit. He wanted to do something. He wanted to know. As the sun spread its light, he heard a whistle from not far off, a light sound, barely more than the last breath of air passing one's teeth.

"I'm on my way in. Don't shoot me," Char said in a low voice that only Terry could hear.

"She's back," Terry said, breathing a sigh of relief. Nightwatch had moved back into the OP. Jim and Devlin were to the sides, faced outboard with rifles at the ready, while Mark kept his eyes fixed on Ivan, looking for any early warning. Terry would have been pacing if he thought he could stand without being seen.

Char crouched as she worked her way between two low mounds on the east side of the impromptu camp. She'd passed the hobbled horses on the way as they continued to graze the scrub. Clyde yipped in excitement at the return of his alpha, but Terry grabbed him quickly by the scruff of the neck so he and Char could pet him and keep him from giving away their position.

"They know we're here," she started, then picked up a stick. "They're set up on this side of the road, in a line, like this." She drew in the dirt. Terry expanded the diagram and built a full map showing their position and what they knew of the enemy.

"Maybe fifteen men. Could be thirty. Armed with AKs, which tells me that it's Sawyer Brown. I didn't see him, so I can't tell you where he is. I'm sorry," she ended. Terry looked at his map and asked Char to adjust the scale so he could better visualize a way to hit them.

"How long do you think it would take us, trying to move silently, to get behind them?" Terry asked. Char looked at the ground and back at the scrub from which she'd recently emerged.

"An hour, maybe more?"

Terry exhaled heavily.

"I think they'll figure something out by then," Terry said slowly, thinking as he went. He loved the sand table exercises in the Marine Corps because they taught him how to plan better, use everything available to keep his people as safe as possible while completing the mission. Usually, it was the destruction of the enemy.

It wouldn't be any different this time.

"What do you think, Char? They gonna fall for the same routine as last time?" She laughed and shook her head.

"Not a chance, TH. So, I'm guessing that's exactly what we're going to do. Maybe having Clyde with us, they'll be more congenial, and won't shoot first," she suggested.

The morning was cool, but not cold. The smell of sage filled the air, with no trace of smoke from the fire remaining. The sun was split on the horizon as it lifted toward a cloudless sky.

"Mark, call Ivan to us," Terry ordered with the plan firmly in his mind. When the four men gathered, he told them what they needed to do and sent them into the scrub with a warning to stay low and not be seen.

Terry and Char started the fire and heated their pot for one last cup of their brew before this started. Terry stood and played fetch with Clyde for a little while, stealing glances back toward the road. He ran up a mound to skyline himself as he and Clyde continued to play.

Then they returned to the fire, ate a little cold breakfast with a hot cup, then covered the fire. Terry checked his rifle, loading one magazine with all seventeen rounds, as much as it would hold before he thought the spring would fail. He looked at his pistol. Only two shots. He put it back in its pouch at his chest as he continued to study the map.

He picked a point about five hundred yards from where Sawyer's men were situated. He and Char would enter the road in the relative safety of distance. An AK-47 was no good at that range, neither was Terry's M4, because of the short barrel, but it was better than the Russian weapon and ammunition. That was the only edge he had.

Well, not the only edge. He and Char were both far more deadly than any of Sawyer Brown's boys, or the big man himself, as long as they were close enough.

"That guy is a fucking putz, don't you think?" Terry asked Char as they stood on the road, waiting. It had been thirty minutes since the rest of the Force headed into the wasteland. They needed to kill another thirty minutes or more until the others were in position.

"We need to distract the men, you say?" Char said, pushing Terry playfully as she removed her shirt and danced around him.

"That's not really what I had in mind," he said, reminding himself that she was a Werewolf. She stripped completely bare and launched herself at Terry. He caught her as he started to fall, then staggered a couple steps and went into the nearby ditch.

Char lifted her head and looked back down the road. "There he is," she said.

"Sawyer Brown?" She nodded. Terry peeked over her bare shoulder and saw the big man's head sticking up. "It's no surprise that he likes a peep show. Damn, you're hot!"

"Well, well, now, TH. And here I was thinking you hadn't noticed," Char cooed.

"No!" Terry exclaimed. "Like, burn my chin on your shoulder hot. How are we going to get your clothes back on you?"

"Isn't that sexy man talk," Char purred. "I brought them with me because I figured you wouldn't be any fun."

Terry was mad that he hadn't seen everything she was doing. She was already two steps ahead of him by showing him where Sawyer Brown was. "So how long do you think they'll be watching us do it in here?" Terry asked. Char kneeled and bounced, giving the boys a bit of a show. They were all more than a quarter of a mile away and couldn't see much, but she was holding their attention as Terry watched one head after another pop out from behind Sawyer.

"Are you fast or slow, Terry Henry Walton? Can you keep me interested for thirty full minutes?" Terry had a hard time answering as perfect breasts bounced in front of his face while he tried to see past them.

"Do you have any inhibitions?" Terry asked, wishing he had binoculars to better see the enemy ahead.

"None," Char replied simply. She nestled down slowly, then put her clothes on. The entire time, Clyde stayed in the road. He was lying down, head between his paws, looking bored as he watched his pack. The humans remained in the ditch until Clyde ran up the road to do his business.

"Clyde!" Terry yelled.

"Clyde!" came an answer from ahead. Sawyer Brown had had enough. The big man was standing in the ditch, hands cupped around his mouth as he called to his dog.

"Showtime," Terry said and stepped into the road. Char joined him and side by side, they walked slowly forward. Clyde was torn. He had eaten well when he was with the man ahead, could feel that he was loved, but he had all those things in his new pack, too. The big difference was that his new alpha was superior.

In all ways.

Clyde turned and trotted back to join Terry and Char, taking his place between them. They stopped.

"What the hell are you feeding that dog?" Char asked, as they were dangerously close to Clyde's business.

Terry had a hard time not looking at the she-wolf, as if she were one to talk.

Sawyer Brown raised his rifle and fired. The round whizzed by, closer than Terry was comfortable with. He dove left and Char went right. Terry stayed out of the ditch, and in the prone position, he sighted in on the big man's chest, raised his aiming point to Sawyer's face, and squeezed.

Sawyer Brown dove back into the ditch, once he realized he was skylined.

Terry relaxed the pressure on the trigger and rotated the lever to "safe," having not fired the weapon. He blinked his eyes clear and scanned the road and fields ahead. No targets. Terry pounded the pavement with a fist. "Dammit!" he growled. He'd missed his chance.

"Now what do we do?" Char asked, fresh out of ideas.

"Talk?" Terry suggested. He stood and moved back to the middle of the road, but this time, he held his rifle at the ready, barrel pointed down the road, finger on the trigger and thumb on the selector lever.

"Sawyer Brown! Let's talk like men!" Terry bellowed. "No one has to die today," he added.

"Just you two," the big man answered from the safety of his hole.

"That could put a crimp in our conversation, Sawyer Brown. I think I have something you need to hear. I know something you don't know!" Terry prompted.

"That's your plan?" Char whispered. "Quoting *The Princess Bride*?" Terry looked at her as she finally gave more insight into her age and showed her excellent taste in movies from the before time.

"No," he countered, although that was exactly what he was doing.

"Send the woman to me!" Sawyer called back. Char started walking.

"Hey! Where are you going?" Terry asked.

"I'm going to go kill him now. That is what you want, right?" She looked confused.

"Yes, but you're not going alone," Terry said, not taking his eyes off the top of Sawyer Brown's head. It wasn't enough to take a shot, but close.

The shooting started from the field and scrub to Terry's left, beyond the enemy lines. His men yelled and fired, but stayed hidden. Terry couldn't see anything that was going on. Sawyer raised his head and turned, looking at the skirmish behind him. Terry dropped to one knee and fired.

Sawyer went down. Terry started running toward the battle with Char and Clyde running close behind. The incoming fire from his right drove him off the road and into the ditch on the left side of the road. Char disappeared into the weeds to the right. Terry shot one man who was more exuberant than the others, thinking that he'd hit his target because Terry and Char both disappeared as if they'd been shot.

That man died without ever knowing what hit him. The other men ducked and fired unaimed shots as they kept their heads down. Terry was able to pick off one more before they stopped firing and stayed hidden.

A couple voices to Terry's left were yelling that they surrendered. The firing stopped completely. Terry continued down the ditch, half-crouched, when Sawyer Brown popped up and fired, hitting Terry in the chest and knocking him over backwards.

Two shots were fired from the field and Sawyer's head exploded in a shower of gore. Clyde brayed as he dove into the ditch after the injured member of his pack, but stopped when Terry scratched him behind the ears.

He sat up and looked. "Well, God damn, would you look at that? That old .45 saved my life." The round from Sawyer's AK had hit the frame, destroying Terry's treasured Colt and giving him a healthy bruise on his chest.

But he lived to fight another day, or at least a few more minutes. His reverie was brief as weapons fire erupted from the right side of the road.

CHAPTER SEVENTEEN

Char surprised the man that anchored the line on the right side of the road. She killed him with a punch that caved in his skull. She grabbed his rifle as the next man down turned to face her. She shot him and started running, shooting the next two in rapid succession before return fire started.

She was hit twice, once in the leg and once in the chest. She went down and rolled behind cover. Char started to heal immediately, but needed more food. She crawled to the men she'd already killed and was surprised that they had nothing on them. Char thought about it for a second and decided against it. She'd recover without eating any of the humans. She denied Marcus before when he insisted and even now, with necessity calling, she couldn't do it. She would never do it. It would simply take more time to heal and that was that.

Dammit, TH, you've made me the damsel in distress and I

hate that shit, she thought as she kept the rifle trained toward the mounds that hid her enemies as they pointed their rifles in her direction.

She waited for someone to come.

❖ ❖ ❖

Terry peeked from the cover of the ditch and saw his four men rounding up the survivors in the field to his left. To his right, no one was visible.

"It's over! Sawyer Brown is dead. Come out with your hands up and you won't be harmed," Terry yelled, unwilling to expose himself.

"Come on out, boys! It's over," Jagoff yelled as he walked from the field, hands on top of his head. Jim carried an armload of rifles, while Ivan struggled with bags of magazines filled with ammunition. Devlin and Mark watched four of Sawyer's men as they walked slowly across the field. "Come on! Hands up and get out here!"

Seven men slowly rose with their hands held out before them.

"Char! Come on out," Terry called as he carefully climbed from the ditch. Clyde was checking out his former master. He peed near the man's head and then ran around to the other members of Sawyer's small army.

Terry watched the dog, saw who he liked and noted that.

Terry made his way through the ditch and accosted the first person he came across. "Where is she?" he demanded. The man pointed toward the east. Terry turned to cover the people who surrendered as he moved away from them. When they walked onto the road and Devlin took charge of the newcomers, Terry ran in the direction the man pointed.

He followed the dead bodies until he found Char, sitting behind a mound with a rifle across her lap. He saw the two holes in her clothing and the blood. Her eyes were closed. He kneeled next to her, putting his fingers on her neck and feeling for the pulse. Char's skin was hot and her pulse was strong. "Thank God," he whispered.

"Ah, you'd miss me," Char said with her eyes still closed. "I'm fine, just a little tired is all." She opened her eyes to see Terry looking at the two bullet holes in her clothes.

"Near misses," she said. He smirked and helped her to her feet. She stretched and flexed, took a deep breath and declared herself one hundred percent. Terry watched her walk stiffly toward the road.

"Private," Terry called to Char. She looked at him with one eyebrow raised and her hands up. "Gather up these weapons and ammunition and bring them to the road," he ordered and strode briskly away without seeing the look of surprise on her face.

The four members of the FDG had eleven prisoners. He looked for the man who told everyone to surrender, the man that Clyde seemed to like. "You, what's your name?"

"They call me Jagoff…" he said, hanging his head.

"Say what? I asked what your name was, and I don't want any bullshit," Terry clarified.

"James, my name is James." The man smiled sheepishly. It had probably been too long since he had heard his own name.

"Well, James, I'm going to be honest in that I have no idea what to do with all of you. What do you think we should do?" Terry asked.

"We're not your enemy, mister. He was." James pointed at Sawyer Brown's corpse.

"Yes, that reminds me. An old tradition of mine is to give a bottle of twenty-year old, or older, single malt scotch to the team member who took out the target. Since we don't have any of that, one of my first bottles of beer to the man who shot Sawyer Brown! Was that you, Mark?" Terry asked, looking at his corporal. Mark shook his head and pointed to James.

"You?"

"It was well past the time that he needed to go, but he kept us fed, gave us purpose. I'm not sorry to see him dead, though, not sorry at all," James said and spit in the direction of the corpse. The others followed suit.

"I really hope that when I die, no one spits on me. So back to my question, James. What do we do now?" James looked to the others and it seemed like some of them wanted to talk, but hesitated.

"What do you guys think?" Terry asked Mark and Devlin. Jim and Ivan were quagmired in trying to get the weapons and ammunition under control. It looked like Jim and Ivan were losing.

"Whatever you decide, sir," Devlin replied quickly. Terry looked to Mark.

"I'm pretty sure I don't want to spend the rest of my days guarding prisoners," Mark offered ambiguously. Terry rolled his finger hoping to get more. "We need friends, not enemies," Mark added helpfully.

Char walked up, glaring at Terry as she struggled with an armload of cumbersome rifles and two packs bursting with ammunition. She unceremoniously dumped it on the ground at Terry's feet and stood there with her arms crossed.

Terry didn't want to push any more of her buttons. He could tell she was still in pain and needed a break. Terry pulled his last bundle of venison jerky from a pocket and handed it to her. "Thanks, Char. Go get Sawyer's belt and pistols. I think they'll look good on you," he started, then hesitated. "You look dogged, take a break and get something to eat." It wasn't an order. He didn't work that way. He cared about his people, but wanted them to take care of themselves. His job was to give them space to do that.

She chuckled. Dogged. That was it. She ran a hand down his arm as she walked past, taking Clyde with her to find a spot in the ditch a short way off, to sit and relax, eat and recover.

"You. It looks like you had something to say," Terry asked.

A man who seemed to be Mark's age spoke out after looking to the others for confirmation. "We have people back in our town. We have to go back for them," he said, sounding desperate.

Terry nodded, then decided.

"Here's what I can offer. To the north, it's a bit of a hike, but up there, we have a town where we're growing more food than we need. What we don't have is enough manpower to work everything that needs worked. We even have power, electrical power, and those of you with any knowledge of that sort of thing could find more work than you can do. We're bringing civilization back to the world. Would you like to join us? It's going to be a great trip, but there's some work to do between now and then." Terry let it hang.

"Talk among yourselves and see what you'd like to do. If we need to go back for the rest of your people, we'll do that and it'll take as long as it takes. I hate to uproot your whole society, but we can't sustain two communities, not right now anyway. Join us and we'll do right by you as long as you do right by us."

James huddled the people together and Terry watched. He understood the lessons from history only too well. When you enforced your power at the end of a gun, when that gun was gone, you found out the people had zero loyalty, only fear. North Korea had existed that way, so it atrophied and the people suffered. When the Chinese liberation came, even communism gave the North Koreans more freedom and liberty than they'd ever had before.

There's no limit to what people will do for you when they believe. Terry hadn't promised them a rose garden and they seemed okay with that. He doubted any of them were allergic to hard work. These people were survivors.

Just like him. Just like Char. Just like all of them.

❖ ❖ ❖

It took two days for the mob to make their way back to town. All of the weapons and provisions were loaded on the horses and everyone walked, including the FDG. Terry wouldn't have it any other way. He and Char hunted to provide meat for the seventeen of them. They ate well and they talked a lot.

As usual, when the people got to know each other, they realized that they had far more in common than not. Once they realized that Terry Henry Walton had no interest in lording his power over them, they relaxed and acted as friends.

He regaled them with stories from books he'd read, revealing very little about himself while keeping the group entertained. The trip went quickly because they didn't push. Terry estimated that they traveled some thirty-five miles.

Not bad for two days.

To everyone's surprise, when told of the opportunity to live with food, clean water, and power, the rest of the town rose to the occasion and packed up. In two more days, they were ready to go.

Terry had too much stuff and no way to carry it all. He searched his memory for something that would be useful, finally settling on the travois, as used by Native Americans centuries before. They strapped blankets across two poles that would be tied to the saddle and the main contraption would drag behind the horse. It was easier than trying to carry everything and would vastly increase what the people could take.

They built four travois and that was where they loaded the weapons and ammunition, blankets, food, and some water. Those with children would ride some of the way.

Terry pulled James aside. "Have you been down to Colorado Springs, or maybe Falcon?" James shrugged, unsure of what Terry was digging for.

"I'm looking for where they hid their weapons after the fall. If we're going to rebuild this nation, we need to make sure that no one else has access to weaponry. Peace through superior firepower, eh?" Terry prodded. "Where'd you get the AKs and all the ammunition?"

"Probably the kind of place you're looking for. Right here in this town, there was a vault and Sawyer Brown found a way in. It was loaded with those rifles and closets completely filled with ammunition. Sawyer didn't let us waste it, but we had as much as we needed whenever we needed it."

"Show me..."

James and Terry walked through the dusty old town and found the bunker tucked behind the last building. It looked like a fruit cellar, but had a door like a bank vault. Whatever Sawyer did to get inside, it paid a huge dividend. They'd been set for fifteen of the past twenty years.

Terry did a quick inventory and as much as he wanted it to be something else, he determined that it was simply a private collection that someone had amassed in the years leading up to the World's Worst Day Ever. This was all surplus gear, rifles from a broad range of eastern bloc countries. Ammunition by all manufacturers. There were only a couple rifles remaining in the vault. Sawyer Brown had pulled out all stops in his effort to eliminate Terry Henry Walton and the FDG.

"Build two more travois and take all this with us. We can't leave it for someone else to find." Terry liked seeing the ammunition. Even if he didn't find the hidden stockpile he knew had to be there, he had enough arms and ammunition to start and win a war of the wasteland.

But that wasn't good enough for TH. He wanted to search for the stockpile. He hunted Mark down to let him know. "You take this group back to New Boulder. Char and I are going to search for the stockpile," Terry informed him.

Mark was instantly boiling mad. "That's bullshit!" he yelled. "You sell these people on a better world, and then you bail on them? You're not going anywhere except back north with us. Do you understand me?" Mark crossed his arms and stood with feet spread wide.

"That's not how it works. I give the orders, and you follow them," Terry said coldly.

"Is your white whale out there somewhere, Terry Henry Walton? I'm begging you, come with us. Search for your mystical Nirvana later." Mark's eyes were wide as he unfolded his arms and clasped his hands in front of him, pleading with Terry to change his mind.

"Can't you take them on your own?" Terry asked.

"Of course I can, but it's not about that. It's about you being the leader we need you to be, the person who's going to bring civilization back to us. I can take them to New Boulder, but I can't do the rest of it. That's you, bastard," Mark said, gaining confidence in being an upstart.

"Fuck me …" Terry hung his head and looked at the ground. Char slapped him on the back while Clyde nuzzled his leg. The people watched, wondering what he was going to do.

THE END

OF

NOMAD FOUND

Terry Henry Walton will return
in Nomad Redeemed, January 2017

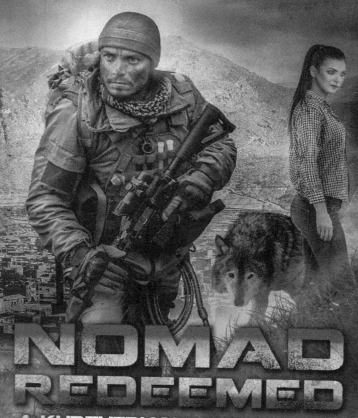

CRAIG MARTELLE
MICHAEL ANDERLE

NOMAD
REDEEMED

A KURTHERIAN GAMBIT SERIES
TERRY HENRY WALTON CHRONICLES
BOOK 2

NOMAD REDEEMED: CHAPTER ONE

The mountain lion wanted the deer as much as Sawyer Brown's people, two men tried to push him away, but he snarled and slashed with a paw at their meager walking sticks. He grabbed the carcass and started to drag it backwards away from the offending humans. The people watched, helplessly. One man was running from the front of the long, drawn out line of people and another two from the back. The two from the back were closing at an unnatural speed.

Terry Henry Walton and Charumati ran straight for the deer, wondering where Mark had disappeared to after shooting the animal, leaving the poor people from Brownsville to fend for themselves.

Terry stopped at fifty yards away and dropped to a knee. As he aimed his M4 combat rifle, Char continued to run past, heading straight for the mountain lion. She veered out of his line of sight for an instant, all he needed to pull the trigger. The round hit the great creature between the eyes as it released the deer and prepared to fight the Werewolf. Char leapt and landed on the thing as it dropped dead.

She growled her dismay at not getting to fight her fellow predator, but she quickly relaxed. As far as she knew, her secret of being a Werewolf was safe. She didn't know that Terry risked hitting her to help her keep that secret.

She stood up and brushed herself off, suggesting they skin

the mountain lion and keep the hide. There was always something to be done with such a magnificent hide.

"So, you decided that fighting a mountain lion bare handed was your best course of action? Is there any reason to carry pistols if you're not going to use them?" Terry asked sarcastically. Sometimes he wondered how hard she was trying.

"Oh, those. I didn't need those to fight that little thing," she replied innocently. The others started cleaning the deer and one man looked proud that he was the one given the opportunity to skin a mountain lion.

When Devlin arrived, out of breath from his run, he was happy that no one got hurt, but he was miffed at having run all that way for no reason.

"Where in the hell did Mark go? He should have been here," Terry stormed, not at Devlin, but he was angry.

"Squirts," Devlin answered, keeping his voice low and shrugging. He knew Terry wasn't mad at him. He turned and jogged slowly back toward the front of the line.

"Break!" Terry yelled in his Marine voice, projecting well past the running man. The people stopped walking and found places to sit. Devlin looked back, shaking his head as Terry smiled.

Mark finally appeared and he looked miserable. There was nothing anyone could do for him. He must have eaten something undercooked or gotten water that was bad. It would pass with enough good water and better food, like the venison they were cutting up.

Terry Henry remained gloomy as they walked north, toward New Boulder. Char stayed by his side and laughed the entire time because TH didn't get his way. Clyde seemed indifferent to it all and was more than happy to feast on mountain lion meat. Terry thought it would be inedible, but this was the wasteland and food was hard to come by.

He asked the man skinning it to do a proper job and cut up the meat as well. The man did as he was told.

Terry told another pair of young men to build a fire that they could use to cook the meat. There wasn't any firewood handy so they conscripted a few other people in search of anything that would burn.

As they returned with bits and pieces of wasteland scrub, Terry helped the men build a field smoker. He stole a blanket that was on the travois, hoping it wasn't someone's bed roll. It would help contain the smoke and that would preserve the meat long enough that they didn't have to eat it at one sitting, although they were getting low on food. A total of thirty six people and twelve horses were headed north on a trip over 100 miles, most of which was through the wastelands east of Denver.

The wastelands weren't as bad as they used to be, some people thought. Terry had lived out there, he knew all about it.

For a while anyway, if you call what he did living.

And he agreed. The climate was changing, getting a little cooler with each year. Terry preferred to think of it as less brutal.

Terry stood and walked the line of people, stroking the grazing horses' necks as he passed. They waved and greeted him kindly. He shook hands and looked at them like refugees, but they weren't. He'd told them that there was work, a new and better life that they could make for themselves.

He hoped Billy Spires saw things that way. Terry decided to ride ahead and make his own luck by preparing Billy and New Boulder for the influx of refugees…

AUTHOR'S NOTES - CRAIG MARTELLE

Written: December 18, 2016

What's there to say? Writing is work, but fun work. The best part of being an author is meeting all the great people out there, other authors, like Michael Anderle, and then all the readers. It is a truly great adventure.

I want to thank Michael for allowing me into the Kurtherian Gambit universe to take a look at things on earth while Bethany Anne was away. After the world's worst day ever happened and everything changed – the apocalypse, Armageddon, whatever you want to call it. Please people, don't let that day happen!

I want to thank those who helped make this book the best it could possibly be. My editor is simply fantastic – Mia Darien has helped me to improve my writing through her comments and consistent correction of my bad punctuation and capitalization. I used to be good at that stuff, but getting quagmired in my own stories, I've lost the edge. My teachers from high school would be appalled.

Kat Lind, Diane Velasquez, and Dorene Johnson are constant companions on the journey. I run an awful lot by them to get their input on how the snippet resonates, either emotionally or visually. I usually only give them a small part of the story and it is in draft form, too. I can't believe they even read it as the first draft is not great! I write better because of these stellar people!

Shout out to the one nicknamed Nomad, Norman Meredith. I loved the name and the visual one gets, so that's what I decided to call this series. Andrew Dobell made the title text pop, too, making it even better.

And then there's Michael Anderle – he is the James Patterson of the science fiction and fantasy world! His understanding of what makes a good plot and character build up is what has made his Kurtherian Gambit series a perpetual bestseller. I am thrilled to get his mentoring as we move forward with Terry Henry Walton's story.

I also want to drop a few good words for Tammy Randolph, right here in Fairbanks. She invited me to talk with a reading group that loves my End Times Alaska series. That was the first time I've ever talked to a group about my books. She made it easy for me to talk with a fairly large group. They were all so kind and it could not have been a better evening for me. Thank you very much – those things keep writers writing.

❖ ❖ ❖

If you liked this story, you might like some of my other books. You can join my mailing list by dropping by my website www.craigmartelle.com or if you have any comments, shoot me a note at craig@craigmartelle.com. I am always happy to hear from people who've read my work. I try to answer every email I receive.

If you liked the story, please write a short review for me on Amazon. I greatly appreciate any kind words, even one or two sentences go a long way. The number of reviews an ebook receives greatly improves how well an ebook does on Amazon.

Amazon – www.amazon.com/author/craigmartelle
Facebook – www.facebook.com/authorcraigmartelle
My web page – www.craigmartelle.com
Twitter – www.twitter.com/rick_banik

Thank you for reading Nomad Found!

AUTHOR'S NOTES - MICHAEL ANDERLE

Written: December 18, 2016

As always, can I say with a HUGE amount of appreciation how much it means to me that you not only read this book, but you are reading these notes as well?

When I started thinking about my fans (and the damned pitchforks and matches - Yikes!) I realized I couldn't write it all.

Not cause I didn't have the time (which I really don't) but I'm not made to write all of the stories. Why? Because some of the genres aren't my specialty.

Now, I knew that Bethany Anne and Michael would be apart for a long time. But, I knew that fans would be asking me, "What the hell happened between book 14/15 and when Michael's came out?"

Am I omniscient? Well, in one word.

No.

Not even remotely. However, I am pretty good at paying attention to what happens in the past and figuring it might happen again. So, when the big honking expanse of years opened up, I was guessing I would get ahead of you fans and get something going. Because (*see above*) pitchforks and matches, man!

They keep an author writing… Or at least running and dodging… something!

So, we get back to the years after Bethany Anne leaves, and the WWDE happens.

(World's Worst Day Ever ... We have an internal document researched and written for us authors by ... -Well, let's say a person in an appropriate career that reviews official reports on what is expected. We will share this at some point in the future, and the author if possible. (I don't know if I can say who it is, due to constraints placed on him.))

Now, we have a post-apocalyptic society and we need to bring some semblance of civilization back for Michael. If anyone here knows me, you know I am not a prepper. My idea of prepping is calling ahead for reservations at a restaurant. If that day happens? I'm going to be heading to my brother's house in central Texas, hoping he doesn't accidentally shoot us because the guy driving (me) doesn't have a tan.

(I can see it now: Picture the scene, a car is coming up the long dirt driveway and stops. The driver gets out yelling, "Paul? Paul? It's me... " Pow ZIIING! The guy starts jumping around, a hand holding his baseball cap on, "He's Shooting, He's SHOOTING!")

Anyway, I told you all of that to say I'm *not* the right guy to write Post-Apoc. However, I KNEW someone who could do it. Why? (Well, I knew him because of 20Books, I knew he could DO it because he already had a successful series set in the Alaskan Wilderness that he sold to a traditional publishing house... pretty good street cred. Well, if you ignore his US Marines experience and other stuff. By other stuff, I'm puposefully ignoring his Legal (lawyer) cred.)

So, I pinged him on Facebook and asked him if he would be interested. Then, I swallowed my ego hard and asked if he would mind taking a character (secondary, or even tertiary character) that was in a couple of the books and use him?

I was concerned he wouldn't like the character at all.

Damned if he didn't say yes! WOOHOO I tell you, WOOHOO :-)

It has been a real pleasure to read the story that Craig has concocted from our discussions. Plus, with Char and the others (even that damned Billy - who SO deserves Felicity, it's awesome.) I'm having a blast learning who is who, and how is the team he's building molding together?

The Terry Henry Walton Chronicles is the First Kurtherian Gambit series to be fronted by a male character (it will beat Michael's book out by three or four days) and I could not be happier. I've heard the first bit on audio for the characters.

It's all going to *rock*.

Stay tuned, book 02 is out in a few weeks!

Best Regards,
Michael Anderle

COMING JANUARY/FEBRUARY 2017

NEVER SUBMIT

THE KURTHERIAN GAMBIT 15

MICHAEL ANDERLE

Made in the USA
Las Vegas, NV
21 June 2024

91336803R00129